CHARLIE SMALL JOURNAL 10: LAND OF THE REMOTOSAURS
A RED FOX BOOK 978 1 782 95327 2

First published in Great Britain by David Fickling Books
when an imprint of Random House Children's Publishers UK
A Penguin Random House Company

David Fickling Books edition published 2010
Red Fox edition published 2015

1 3 5 7 9 10 8 6 4 2

Penguin Random House is committed to a sustainable future for our business, our readers
and our planet. This book is made from Forest Stewardship Council® certified paper.

MIX
Paper from
responsible sources
FSC® C018179

Set in 15/17pt Garamond MT

Red Fox Books are published by Random House Children's Publishers UK,
61–63 Uxbridge Road, London W5 5SA

www.randomhousechildrens.co.uk
www.totallyrandombooks.co.uk
www.randomhouse.co.uk

Addresses for companies within The Random House Group Limited can be found at:
www.randomhouse.co.uk/offices.htm

THE RANDOM HOUSE GROUP Limited Reg. No. 954009

A CIP catalogue record for this book is available from the British Library.

Printed and bound in Great Britain by Clays Ltd, St Ives plc

PUBLISHER'S NOTE

This is the tenth volume of Charlie Small's amazing journal. An eight-year-old boy found it in a new computer game he'd been given for his birthday; inside the box was a disc, but instead of the game booklet he found a battered and torn notebook with loose bits of paper and dry, yellowing leaves hanging out. *What a rip-off!* he thought, but when he had a closer look he realized it was a brand new Charlie Small journal. He sent it straight to the publisher without delay, and now you can read the most exciting Charlie Small book so far.

There must be other notebooks to find, so please keep your eyes peeled. If you do come across an amazing diary, or see an eight-year-old boy wearing a black sweatshirt with a yellow lightning-bolt logo, please let us know at the website: **www.charliesmall.co.uk**

Mr Nickelodious

Trumpery Ward

GENTLEMAN EXPLORER AND
CUSTODIAN OF THE CHARLIE SMALL JOURNALS

NAME: Charlie Small

ADDRESS: Land of the Remotosaurs

AGE: 400!

MOBILE: 07713 123

SCHOOL: The only school I go to is the school of adventures

THINGS I LIKE: Jakeman, Philly and their Space Balloon; Spriggot; Hock and the Bush Pigs

THINGS I HATE: Remotosaurs; Vampire Sparrows; Nemesis Gamer

If you find this book, PLEASE look after it. This is the ONLY true account of my remarkable adventures.

My name is Charlie Small and I am four hundred years old, maybe even more. But in all those long years I have never grown up. Something happened when I was eight years old, something I can't begin to understand. I went on a journey... and I'm still trying to find my way home. Now, although I've played the deadliest computer game ever, been attacked by auto-creatures from the beginning of time and nearly zapped by someone just like YOU, I still look like any eight-year-old boy you might pass in the street.

I've destroyed dinosaurs and come face to face with the terrifying Gamer. You may think this sounds fantastic, you could think it's a lie, but you would be wrong. Because EVERYTHING IN THIS BOOK IS TRUE. Believe this single fact and you can share the most incredible journey ever experienced.

Charlie Small

Another World!

'Caw, caw, caw!'

The faint sound of animal calls coming from outside woke me and I slowly opened my eyes. Bright sunlight was pouring through the slit of a window.

Where the heck am I? I wondered. Then I remembered, and in a flash I rolled off the bench I'd been sleeping on and crouched on the floor, ready to spring into action if any unfriendly creatures had joined me in the night. But no – the room was deserted and, apart from the high-pitched calls coming from outside, everything was silent.

I hurried over and looked out of the window to get some idea of where I was.

'Oh boy, what a view!' I exclaimed as a shiver of wonder and fear rippled down my spine.

I looked down on to the strangest sight. I've

This is the view from the window
(The window was longer than this but I couldn't fit it on the page!)

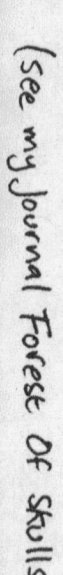
(see my Journal Forest Of Skulls)

been in plenty of woods before but this place was like something from a gothic fairytale. It was about the size of twenty football pitches, and completely enclosed by a circle of towering cliffs. Half the area was covered with a dark dense jungle of magnificent giant redwoods, their jagged tops only five metres below me. Sinuous creepers wound themselves like emerald snakes through the branches of the enormous trees. Some gnarled trunks, bare of any foliage, soared above the rest and lichen hung like swathes of fur from the boughs. Greasy black ravens perched amongst dripping, needle-like leaves.

A thick mist rising from the depths of the

forest gave the scene a dream-like quality. It was like looking at a landscape from the beginning of time.

Where the heck have I landed up now? I wondered. It was all rather confusing. After all, it was only a few hours ago I'd been face to face with a snarling, cold-eyed Tyrannosaurus Rex! No, really – it's true. I have had the most extraordinary time . . .

A Dino Disagreement!

After escaping from a planet of ghastly Gerks with my new pals, Theo and Harmonia Jakeman, I slipped and fell from their wonderful Space Balloon, tumbling towards the ground hundreds of metres below.

Down and down I dropped – straight into ten tonnes of snarling trouble. A thumping, grunting monster tracked me through the night and I crawled into a cave in a high cliff to hide. At the back of the cave I found a tall, frozen waterfall – and entombed inside I could see the hazy outline of an icebound Tyrannosaurus Rex. I tapped nervously on the thick ice sheet, but it was quite dead and I breathed a sigh of relief. I was safe at last.

ROAR! I span round as a monstrous muzzle was thrust into the mouth of the cave. My pursuer had sniffed me out, and by the look of the snapping and salivating jaws, it was *another* T-Rex!

'Yikes!' I cried, pushing myself back against the frozen waterfall and sidling away from the dinosaur's twitching snout. Clouds of steam billowed from his nostrils and his beady eyes stared hungrily at me through the cave's narrow entrance. Suddenly the massive dinosaur rammed his muzzle further into the cave, his scaly lips brushing the leg of my jeans as a fat, purple tongue darted out and licked me from top to toe as if I were an ice cream. I scrambled further away from the beast as his tongue snaked out again, curled around my ankle and began dragging me towards his drooling mouth.

'Gerroff!' I yelled and yanked myself free. Then, as I edged along the back wall I spotted a narrow passage and ducked inside.

RARRR! The monster's roar of frustration echoed around the cave as I ran along the dark tunnel, deeper into the cliff. My heart was

Yikes! The dinosaur licked my face!

pounding and my throat was dry – I'd never seen anything so terrifying in all my adventures.

Suddenly I came to a rusty, cast-iron staircase that climbed up inside the cliff and I cautiously began to tiptoe up the dark flight of steps, my rubber-soled trainers hardly making a sound. *Phew!* It was a long climb, and when I finally reached the top I was panting and wheezing like an old man. In front of me was a large iron door. I carefully pushed the handle down and with a grinding squeal of rusty hinges, the door opened.

squeal!

And that's how I found the room I'm sitting in now. It's a really strange place. There are benches and peg rails along two walls, with a neat row of dark clothing hanging from the hooks. It looks just like the gym changing rooms at school.

Apart from the door that I came in by and a small washroom off to one side, the only other door stands next to the window that looks out onto the weird jungle world. Last night I was so tired after my run-in with the demented dinosaur that I immediately stretched out on one of the wooden benches and, using my rucksack for a rather lumpy pillow, fell into a deep, deep sleep.

Now, writing my journal in the harsh light of morning, it sounds totally crazy – but then *all* of my adventures have been unbelievable. If I want to find out what this weird place is, I'll have to carry on exploring.

Charlie Cool

I've just checked out the peg racks that line the changing room and found a small black uniform hanging from each hook, consisting of an odd-shaped helmet and a sweatshirt with a hard, shell-like chest guard sewn into the front. I tried one on – the top fits me perfectly, but the trousers that come with it are so short I'd look as daft as Tweedledum or Tweedledee if I wore a them!

There was also a wide leather belt that I've strapped around my waist, with a holster on one side holding a shiny blue gun. The gun's a strange shape; it has a tapered, nozzle-like barrel that makes it look like a space-age water pistol.

A really odd-shaped helmet

oh boy, a ray-gun!

Then I did a really stupid thing! Without thinking I pointed the gun at a shoe rack and pulled the trigger. *BOOF!* A thin, red beam shot from the nozzle and sent the shoe rack flying across the room to smash into pieces on the opposite wall. Woops, what a mess! But still, one of these will be really handy if I come across another terrorizing T-Rex.

I've just had a look in the washroom mirror and, even if I say so myself, I look pretty cool! My uniform top is jet-black with a bright yellow flash, like a bolt of lightning, printed on the front. The belt hangs low on my hips like Wild Bob Ffrance's six-shooters and the laser gun glows electric blue in its holster.

I'm ready to tackle whatever the primeval jungle has to offer! I'll write later.

(See my Journal Desking Mountain)

Into The Unknown

Phew — I'm safe now, but it's been an incredible day!

I opened the door onto the balcony and was hit by a cacophony of sound coming from the jungle that echoed around the surrounding cliffs. Ravens cawed, birds twittered and something was crashing about like a berserk bulldozer.

Suddenly a terrifying roar erupted from somewhere amongst the trees — it sounded like that ferocious Tyrannosaurus Rex again. The noisy forest became eerily silent, and I wondered whether it would be safer to go back the way I'd come. But as I thought this I heard the door clunk closed behind me. When I turned to open it I discovered there was no handle on the outside. *Oh, yikes!* I had locked myself out. I tried to prise the door open with my penknife, but it was stuck fast. There was no choice but to climb down into the world below and hope, somewhere, I'd find another route out of this strange place.

I quickly and quietly scuttled down the staircase that zig-zagged back and forth across the cliff face. The light grew dimmer the lower I got and the air became filled with an overpowering smell of woody pine. The forest was still and quiet, as if waiting for something to happen.

I held onto a rail with my right hand and let my left hand brush against the cliff wall. It felt cold and smooth and not like rock at all. I gave it a knock with my knuckles and it rang like a bell – the cliff seemed to be made of metal!

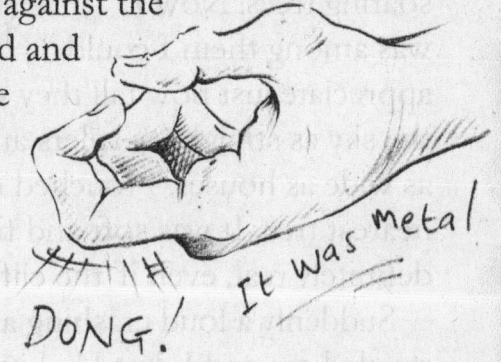

DONG!

It was metal

Now I could see a row of rivet heads joining two huge sections of the cliff together. *This is getting weirder by the minute*, I said to myself.

As I dropped down below the level of the jungle canopy, I kept my eyes peeled and my ears alert for any sign of danger. All I saw were quick, bright flashes as small, rainbow-coloured birds with leathery wings and long, saw-toothed beaks zipped through the trees. Eventually, with legs as wobbly as jelly from the long climb, I reached the bottom.

Looking left and right, I ran across a short, open stretch of ground coated with a thick carpet of pine needles, and dived into the cover of the soaring trees. Now I was among them I could  appreciate just how tall they were, climbing into the sky as straight as rulers and with trunks as wide as houses. I touched the bark of the nearest tree. It was soft and fibrous – these were definitely real, even if the cliffs weren't.

Suddenly a loud crashing amongst the trees startled me and I dived behind a trunk for cover. A vile, sharp-snouted Velociraptor emerged

from the undergrowth. It was the size of a wolfhound and had a large, grinning jaw lined with terrible-looking teeth. I slipped the ray gun from my pocket just in case, but the ferocious beast didn't see me and with a clatter of branches it disappeared deeper into the jungle.

I breathed a sigh of relief and set off in the opposite direction, weaving a path through the trees. The jungle was so dense I wasn't able to keep a straight course and I soon found I was completely lost!

Saw-Toothed Sparrows!

I battled my way through tangles of branches and hanging creepers, unable to see more than a few metres ahead. Trees surrounded me and a huge cliff wall surrounded them; I started to feel like an insect trapped in a jar. Was there a way out from this strange enclosed place? Feeling exhausted, I flopped down on a wide tree stump to rest.

I opened my rucksack, took out the fruit I had left from my trip to Gerkania and bit into the juicy flesh. Yum! It tasted just like a four-cheese pizza, and I gave a loud burp of appreciation. As I sat there chewing and thinking and humming to myself, a brightly-coloured bird came and perched on a nearby branch. It gave a hoarse little squawk that sounded like a hacksaw being drawn across metal.

It was one of the birds I'd spotted on my climb down the cliff face and was an odd little thing, the size of a garden sparrow. The feathers

A funny
little bird
perched on a
nearby branch ↗

on its chest shimmered with all the colours of the rainbow but its drab wings were like thin sheets of grey leather stretched over a bony frame. Its head was as long as its body, and the heavy, bony beak had nasty serrated edges like a kitchen knife. The bird cocked its head on one side and looked at me with small, black, button eyes.

'Hello, who's a pretty boy then?' I said.

'Crrroo,' the bird cooed in reply.

'Do you want some fruit?' I asked, and held out a blob of the juicy pap. The bird cocked its head to the other side and looked at me blankly.

'Here, try some. I won't bite, you silly thing,' I said and gave it a reassuring smile. The razor-billed bird shuffled to the end of the branch and tentatively stretched its beak forward.

'That's right,' I said. 'Here you are.'

SNAP! It struck with the speed of a cobra – but not at the fruit! Its serrated beak clamped onto my finger and the bird hung on, warbling and twittering for all it was worth. My finger felt like it was being crushed in a vice.

'Yeeowza! I cried, dropping the fruit as I tried to shake the critter off. Suddenly the bird let go, leaving my finger with pinpricks of blood all

Yeeeow!

along it. 'You little devil,' I said, blowing on my
throbbing finger to cool it down. 'What did you
do that for?'

The feather-brained pest licked hungrily at a
drop of my blood on its bill and gave an excited
squawk. Uh oh, I had a horrible thought that
maybe it wasn't after the fruit at all – maybe it
was after my blood! Another of the rainbow
birds appeared, perching in the branches
overhead and looking down at me.

'Croop,' it peeped, eyeing me intently.

'Crrroo, craaak, croop!' The bushes all around
suddenly became alive with the bloodthirsty
critters, staring at me with the same blank
expressions. Uh oh, this wasn't good!

With a horrible flutter of dry, leathery wings,
the flock swooped towards me and I was
covered with flapping, pecking vampire birds.

'Get off, you blood-sucking beasts!' I cried as the birds stabbed at the back of my hands, grazing them with their saw-toothed beaks, and pecked at the helmet on my head. In desperation, I grabbed some fallen branches on the ground. They were covered with great clusters of needle-like leaves and, holding one in each hand, I struggled to my feet. With arms outstretched I started to spin as fast as I could, the thick foliage whacking the hovering vampire birds and knocking them off course. They came again but I kept on spinning, windmilling my arms and thwacking the feathered fiends until they flew screeching off into the jungle.

I flopped to the ground feeling sick and dizzy, and sat there for a while to get my breath back. Then, checking the birds had really gone, I climbed shakily to my feet and hurried away.

Touching The Sky

I was soon over my ordeal, but as I continued to weave my way through the giant trees I began to wonder when I would reach the other side. Was the enclosed jungle bigger than it looked? The only sure way to pinpoint my position was to climb to the top of one of the trees.

I chose a massive tree, its trunk as wide as a castle tower rising straight up and disappearing into the leafy canopy overhead. Its bark was soft and pitted and provided perfect footholds, so I jammed the toe of my trainer into a crevice and started climbing. My monkey skills were a bit rusty, but I got the hang of it again and was soon scurrying skyward, using thick creepers that hung from above to help me.

I climbed and climbed, pushing my way through clumps of scratchy fir needles. The air was heavy with a spicy orange scent, and swirled with choking dust motes. Coughing and spluttering, I pushed on, suddenly emerging through the dark green forest roof.

The trunk, now bare of any branches, continued up for another ten metres to a flat, truncated top. I wanted to get the best possible view of the jungle around me, so I continued to climb. As I reached the very top of the tree, I pulled myself up by the last foothold, and *thump*, the helmet on my head bashed against something really hard.

'What the heck?' I gasped, looking up to see

(See my Journal Gorilla City)

what I'd bumped into. There was nothing there! I tried to pull myself onto the flat top again and *thump*; I cracked my head a second time!

'This is ridiculous!' I said out loud. 'There's nothing there but the sky.' I lifted my hand – and touched it. I actually touched the sky!

'Totally weird,' I said, and moved my hand across the cool, smooth surface. Then I realized that it wasn't the sky at all. I tapped my finger against it. Yep, there was no doubt; it was a huge sheet of glass curving right over the jungle from the cliff tops on one side to the cliff tops on the other. The tree I was on, and the other extra-tall trees protruding above the jungle top, were acting as massive supporting pillars.

CRACK!

I cracked my head against something hard!

It was as if I had stumbled into some sort of jungle greenhouse – one that's inhabited by deadly dinosaurs.

A Giant Shock! Fee-fi-fo-fum!

Then the strangest thing happened; a huge human voice suddenly boomed out across the jungle. I looked up and nearly fell from my perch at the top of the tree. To my horror I saw the enormous face of a giant man appearing above me, filling half the sky!

The giant had a thin moustache on his top lip and his mean eyes peered in at me through the glass roof.

'*Cripes*, a gi-giant!' I cried and tried to escape, but I was frozen with fear and couldn't move.

'WHO ARE YOU?' thundered the face.

'I – I – I,' I stammered, little beads of sweat popping onto my forehead and trickling down into my eyes.

'ANSWER ME, YOU MEASLY LITTLE WORM,' the giant yelled, his mouth curling into a nasty sneer. 'ANSWER ME, OR I'LL CRUSH YOU UNDERFOOT!'

'I – I – I,' I stuttered again, my tongue unable to form any words.

'AARGH!' roared the giant and moved as if to make a grab for me; my arms went as weak

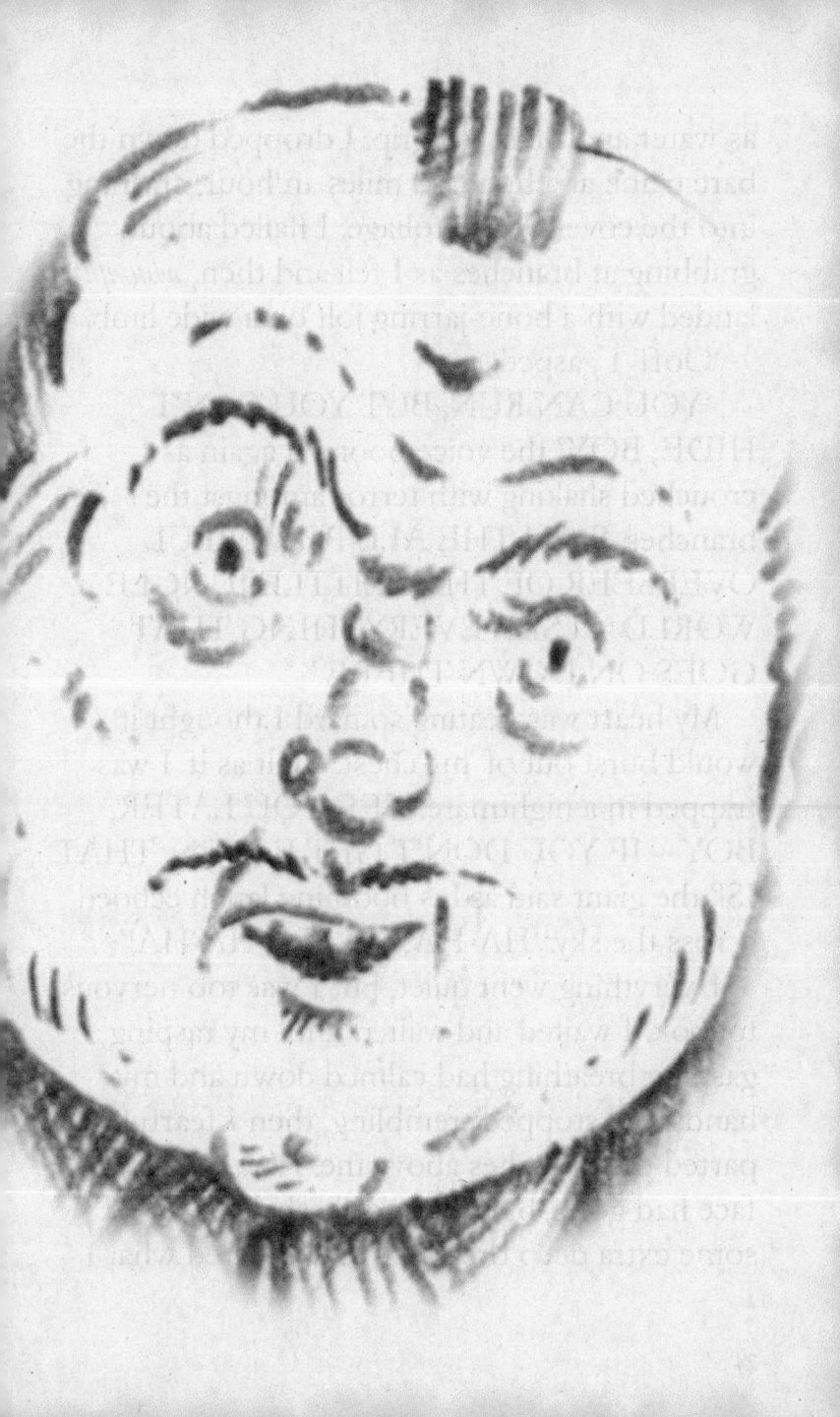

as water and I lost my grip. I dropped down the bare trunk at a hundred miles an hour, crashing into the cover of the foliage. I flailed about, grabbing at branches as I fell and then, *whump!* I landed with a bone-jarring jolt on a wide limb.

'Oof!' I gasped.

'YOU CAN RUN, BUT YOU CAN'T HIDE, BOY,' the voice boomed again as I crouched shaking with terror amongst the branches. 'I AM THE ALL-POWERFUL OVERSEER OF THAT LITTLE JUNGLE WORLD – I SEE EVERYTHING THAT GOES ON DOWN THERE.'

My heart was beating so hard I thought it would burst out of my chest. I felt as if I was trapped in a nightmare. 'SEE YOU LATER, BOY – IF YOU DON'T GET EATEN, THAT IS!' the giant said as his booming laugh echoed across the sky. 'HA-HA, HA-HA, HA-HA!'

Everything went quiet, but I was too nervous to look. I waited and waited until my rasping, gasping breathing had calmed down and my hands had stopped trembling, then I fearfully parted the branches above me. *Phew!* The giant face had gone, but I was really shaken. I took some extra deep breaths and wondered what I should do next. Although the cliffs weren't very far away, it was already getting towards evening and I didn't fancy trekking through the dark with a giant on the loose – I would stay where I was for the night.

I shinned further down the tree looking for a suitable perch, and at the junction of a wide branch discovered a deep, arched recess in the tree's massive trunk. I gratefully crawled inside.

There was a small archway in the trunk

A Place For The Night

As I write up this journal, my mind is spinning with images of dinosaurs and giants. The night is echoing with the whoops and roars of mysterious beasts and I'm so glad I'm not down there with them. I've covered myself with a warm blanket of lichen and feel quite snug and safe; I can snooze here without fear of falling out of the tree.

I've checked my Wild Animal Collector's Cards and found one all about those vicious little birds that attacked me earlier. This is what it has to say:

PREDATOR RATING 14

The Voracious Vampire Bird

Don't be fooled by the small size and pretty colours of the Vampire Bird. It is always hungry and has a ravenous appetite for the blood of any living creature. When they swarm, these rapacious eaters can suck all the blood from an elephant in fifteen minutes! If you see one, don't hang around or you will be drunk dry in a flash.

WILD ANIMAL COLLECTORS CARDS

It's lucky I escaped when I did! I'm very hungry now and first thing in the morning I must look for some decent grub. Then I'll search for a way out of this strange and scary place. Goodnight.

Spriggot

You won't believe what's happened NOW!

When I opened my eyes the next morning, sitting a little way along the branch and staring intently at me was a tiny man about the size of a large garden gnome (about forty centimetres tall). I shut my eyes again – *I must be dreaming*, I thought. But when I opened them a second time, the little man was still there. His face was as brown and wrinkly as a walnut; he had a shock of white hair and was wearing a leather jerkin, breeches and pointed shoes. Perched on the branch next to him was a jet-black raven with a leather harness over its head. The bird was glaring at me with a beady yellow eye.

The tiny man →

This is crazy, I thought. *First I see giants and now elves!* I closed my eyes again. I hadn't believed in fairies since I was about four years old. Then all of a sudden, something sharp and spiky hit me on the head.

'Wake up, why don't ya?' said a thin, vibrating voice that buzzed in the air like the sound of a bee.

I opened my eyes just as a second pine cone hit me on the end of my nose.

'Hey!' I said, my mouth wide open.

'I've bin waitin' fer hours,' the man said crossly. The raven snapped its bill in agreement. 'What's wrong with yer?' said the wrinkled man. 'Close yer mouth. You look as gormless as a cod!'

'Sorry,' I said gormlessly. 'Who are you? *What* are you?'

'Me first,' grumbled the little man. 'Who and what are *you*?'

'I'm Charlie Small,' I said. 'I'm a boy. Are you

an elf or something?'

'An elf?' cried the man. 'How dare you. I'm not an elf or a fairy or a pixie or a will-o-the-wisp. I'm a *sprite*, so there.'

'A sprite – what's a sprite?' I asked.

'I am,' said the man, exasperated. 'I just told ya, didn't I?'

'What's your name?' I asked.

'Spriggot,' said the man. The raven suddenly took off and swooped across to a branch right beside me and, thrusting its head forward, began clacking its long grey beak together like castanets. I recoiled, wary of the bird's snapping bill.

'And that's my raven, Darkness,' continued Spriggot. 'Just give her a tickle. She won't bite.'

I slowly raised an arm and tickled the large black bird on her head. Her eyes closed and she made little croaks of pleasure.

Darkness

'Hello, Darkness,' I cooed feebly.

'Now, if you get out of my doorway, I can get us some breakfast,' said the grouchy sprite.

'Oh, sorry,' I said, scrambling up. 'I didn't realize.'

'That's as may be,' said Spriggot. 'But it is and you've bin blockin' it all night.'

As we changed places, Darkness gave a raucous *caw!* With a flap of her wide wings, she glided over to a platform of twigs on a nearby branch and settled herself down. Spriggot began to sweep away the layer of pine needles where I'd been sitting and lifted a wooden hatchway underneath. He started to descend inside the hollow trunk.

'Come on then, Charlie Small,' he said to me with a wave of his tiny hand.

Breakfast At Spriggot's

Following him was easier said than done. The hatch was designed for a sprite and my bum got wedged in the narrow entrance. I pushed and squeezed and was just about to give up when Spriggot yanked on my legs from below and I popped through the gap.

Luckily, it was quite roomy inside the huge trunk. A spiral of rough steps led down to another platform of wood on which stood a small bed, a little wooden table and a tiny stove. The room was about three metres in diameter and its walls were lined with cupboards and shelves on which stood hand-carved ornaments, dusty books, long pipes full of tobacco and various stuffed woodland creatures. The place smelled of sap and spices and old, tanned leather.

I squatted down by the little table as Spriggot lifted a hatch in this floor.

'Let's see what's in the pantry,' he said and hauled on a creeper that hung down inside the tree. He pulled up a large sack and tipped a pile of fat forest mushrooms, crisp roots and juicy berries into a big pan.

He stoked up the stove, sending smoke billowing along a tubular metal chimney that left the trunk through a hollowed-out branch.

Within minutes the air was filled with the delicious smell of frying mushrooms.

'Now, I expect you know what's goin' on, don't yer?' said Spriggot in his buzzing voice as he stirred the mushrooms and roots.

'What d'you mean, what's goin' on?' I asked, my tummy starting to rumble as he ladled some of the food onto the biggest plate he could find and handed it to me.

'Thanks!' I said. The plate was only the size of a CD, and the fork like something from a toy set, but the food was delicious and surprisingly filling. I waited for the little man to continue as he chewed his breakfast with his gummy jaws.

'What I means is, what's going on with those battling behemoths?' he said at last.

'Be-whats?' I asked with my mouth full.

'Deadly dinosaurs; marauding megaraptors, call 'em what you like, but this place is full of 'em,' growled the sprite.

'*I* don't know what's going on; I was hoping you could tell *me*,' I said. 'I heard lots of roaring in the night, but I've only seen a couple of the critters – oh, and some sort of vampire birds.'

'Oh the bloodsucking sparrows have always

been here. They don't trouble me, though – not enough blood for 'em to bother with. But the monsters are a different matter,' said Spriggot. 'Where did they come from, that's what I want to know? It's gettin' so a harmless sprite can't go about his business without some dastardly dinosaur trying to devour him.'

'The dinosaurs haven't always been here, then?' I asked.

'No way,' buzzed the wrinkled little man, wiping his mouth with his sleeve and letting out a fruity burp. 'I've lived in this ancient woodland for centuries and it's always been a quiet, peaceful, unchanging sort of place. Then one day a crowd of men turned up driving smoke-billowing diggers and cranes and all sorts of clanking contraptions. They started to put up those great metal walls around the trees!'

No Way!

'The cliffs weren't here either?' I asked.

'No they weren't, ugly great things,' huffed Spriggot. 'They took a thousand men a thousand days to build and they've completely spoiled my view.'

'So they *are* man-made then,' I said. 'I thought they felt like metal. Whoever built them must have put the glass roof on too.'

'There's a roof?' gasped the little man.

'Yeah – I wonder if it has something to do with the giant,' I said, thinking out loud.

'Giant? *Giant?* What are you on about, Charlie? Giants only exist in fairytales!' grumbled the exasperated little man.

I could have said the same about sprites, but I kept my mouth closed. 'I saw a giant face peering in through the glass roof,' I explained.

'I don't know nuffin' about no giant,' growled Spriggot. 'All I know is that soon after the cliffs had gone up, the dinosaurs arrived. What's goin' on, Charlie Small?'

'I really have no idea. It's very strange,' I said, wiping my brow where a film of sweat had formed. 'Oh, my goodness; what sort of mushrooms are these?' I'd started to feel very woozy all of a sudden, and my head began to spin.

'There's nothin' wrong with my mushrooms,' snapped Spriggot. 'What's the matter?'

Poisoned! ☠

'I feel all swimmy and hot,' I moaned.

'Uh oh – you didn't get bitten by those vampire birds, did ya?' asked the little man, getting to his feet and feeling my forehead with his tiny hand.

I held up my finger with its row of pinhead scabs.

'You should have told me before,' buzzed Spriggot. 'Them varmints are venomous!'

'Venemous?' I groaned as I started to shiver, feeling suddenly cold. 'It d-d-d-didn't mention that on my collector's card.'

'No wonder you saw giants in the sky – you were hallucinatin'!' said the sprite. 'Now, don't worry, lie down here.' He took me by the hand and pulled me towards the bed. I flopped down. It was much too short for me – but it made a comfortable pillow and I stretched my legs out across the floor. My head was spinning with crazy images, but at least I knew I'd only imagined the giant. That was a relief!

Spriggot hurried over to a corner cupboard and took out a dark brown bottle. 'I have an

antidote,' he said, pulling out the cork.
A strong, musty odour filled the room.

'What is it?' I groaned, sweat popping
out on my forehead again. It smelt like
a mixture of aniseed and cow dung.

'You don't wanna know,' said
Spriggot. 'Here, take a swig. You'll
soon feel better.' I lifted the small bottle to my
lips, swallowed the contents in one gulp and lay
back on the floor.

Oh, yuck, I thought. *That tasted hairy!*
Something was caught in my teeth and I spat it
into my hand. It looked like the feathery leg of a
very fat and juicy spider.

YUCK!

'Gross!' I mumbled.

'Ooh! I wonder how that got in
there,' said Spriggot.

A cooling wave spread through my body and
stars exploded before my eyes like fireworks.
Then, *whoa!* I felt I was sliding down a long,
winding chute at a hundred miles an hour.
Colours pulsed in the air, shifting and changing
as if I was inside a giant kaleidoscope. My head
seemed to spin one way and my tummy another.
Then, *whoosh!* A blast of cold air hit me in the
face, my head cleared and I opened my eyes.

'OK?' buzzed Spriggot, looking concerned.

I sat up and took a deep breath. I still felt very wobbly, but my fever had broken. 'Yeah!' I said. 'Much better. Thanks, Spriggot.'

'Oh, s'nothin',' said the sprite, looking very important and pleased with himself. 'It's just one of the many old sprite remedies handed down to me.'

I tried to get up but my legs felt as if they were filled with jelly.

'You stay there,' ordered the little gnarly man. 'It's gonna take a while to get over a Vampire Bird bite.'

'How long?' I asked. 'I've got to find a way out of this place. I'm trying to get home.'

'Oh, a day or two should do it,' said the sprite. 'In the meantime, you must stay here.'

Spriggot went out and collected armfuls of lichen and made up a bed for me on the floor. After a tiny cup of sweet-smelling hazelnut coffee, I stretched out and fell into a deep sleep full of strange, swirling dreams.

Phoning Home

I've been staying with Spriggot for three days now and I have completely recovered. I'm starting to get restless cooped up inside this tree; it's very cosy, but very cramped for someone of my size. As soon as Spriggot returns, I'll say my cheerios and set off on my journey again.

He is out foraging for food on the back of Darkness. He sits astride the raven's back as she soars through the air, steering her with a small leather harness and reins, catching flying insects in a net and swooping down to the ground to pick mushrooms from jungle clearings.

Last night we sat close to the warm stove, talking about our homes and families. Spriggot is hundreds of years old, just like me, and has lived in this tree for most of his life. Sprites are solitary creatures, living on their own until they get married, usually at the ripe old age of six hundred and forty. It takes them that long because, living in such isolation, they rarely meet another sprite – let alone one they want to marry!

All the talk of family has made me feel a bit

homesick so, while I'm waiting for Spriggot, I'm going to try and phone home . . .

I was surprised to get a connection inside this glass-topped world, but Mum answered the call after just two rings. Her voice was as clear as if she were in the next tree!

'Oh, hello darling, is everything all right?'

'Yes, Mum, everything's fine – apart from being chased by a ferocious Tyrannosaurus Rex, poisoned by a vampire bird and threatened by an imaginary giant,' I replied. 'I'm staying with a sprite in his tree at the moment.'

'Sounds wonderful, dear,' said Mum cheerily. 'Oh, wait a minute, Charlie. Here's your dad just come in. Now remember, don't be late for tea, and if you're passing the shops on the way back, please pick up a pint of milk. Bye.'

'Hope to see you soon, Mum,' I cried, but she had already hung up.

She says the same every time I call. Even if I told her I was being gnawed to pulp by a ginormous polar bear, she would think it 'sounds wonderful'. And she's still expecting me home in time for tea, although I've been gone for four hundred years. Oh well, it's always great to hear Mum's voice, even if she does seem to be stuck in a time warp.

Hello, Spriggot and Darkness have just returned. I'll write more later.

Terrordactyl Attack!

'Home?' cried Spriggot when I told him my plans. 'What do you want ter go home fer?'

'To see my mum and dad,' I explained. 'I don't want to be trapped inside a walled jungle for the rest of time.'

'Why, what's wrong with my home – not good enough for yer? Too scared? There's nothin' to worry about,' said Spriggot. 'We're perfectly safe here.' As he uttered those words, there was an enormous *CRASH*! and the air filled with swirls of choking wood dust as a large, hooked claw ripped through the side of the tree, slicing open a jagged slit in the trunk. *CRASH!* It came again, gouging at the soft, spongey bark. Then, *smack!* The end of a very long beak knifed

through the narrow slit, grabbed
Spriggot and started to pull him
out.

'Help, Charlie!' screamed the
little man, his voice buzzing
like a swarm of wasps.

I picked up the frying pan
and whacked the beak as
hard as I could. The creature
let out a startled squawk, but
didn't release Spriggot. It tried to
pull my struggling friend through the
gap as if it were prising a snail from its
shell. I reached for the ray gun at my waist,
but stopped – I was just as likely to hit the
floundering elf as his attacker.

I quickly shook the rucksack from my back
and groped around in my trusty explorer's kit
for anything that might help. My hand closed
around the plastic lemon and I pulled it
out, flipped open the top and, plunging
my hand dangerously between the
parted mandibles of the huge beak,
squirted a jet of bitter lemon
juice up towards the
creature's gullet.

I expected it to cough and retch as the sour acid hit its throat, but it didn't. Something much more curious happened. *Fizzzzz!* With a sound like crackling electricity and the smell of burning plastic, a tendril of black smoke wafted from its bill.

What's that all about? I wondered as the predator dropped Spriggot, let out an angry squawk and, with a flapping of mighty wings, took off. I ran to the slit and peered out, just in time to see the grey-green, hunched back of a Pterodactyl crashing through the branches overhead. It was as big as a man with wide, membranous wings stretching from its clawed hands to its clawed feet like a wizard's dark cloak. The revolting creature opened its grinning bill and squawked furiously as it flapped off into the clear sky.

'Zuzz!' Spriggot buzzed, getting shakily to his feet. 'Thanks, Charlie!'

Time To Move On

'You can't stay here any more,' I said to the sprite. 'That creature might come back at any time.'

'But this is my house,' said Spriggot, looking round. 'I've lived here for centuries and I'm not leaving just because some prehistoric parrot has moved into the neighbourhood. If it tries it again, I'll wring its neck.'

'And how are you going to do that?' I asked. 'He's five times the size of you.'

'I'll be all right, you'll see. You go on if yer want to, but I'm stayin' here,' said the little man. 'I'm a sprite, a woodland creature and I've not once left this forest in all my life!'

'Well, I've *got* to go on,' I said. 'I'm trying to find my way home and I won't be able to do that until I find a way out of this man-made madhouse.'

'Well, good luck to yer, then,' said Spriggot, his arms folded defiantly across his chest. 'I'm stayin' put.'

'So long then,' I said picking up my rucksack and holding out my hand to the sprite. 'And thanks for everything – the medicine and that.'

'Whatever,' said Spriggot, ignoring my hand.

'I'd like to stay, honest,' I said. 'But I can't.'

'No skin off my nose,' said the sprite. 'So long, Charlie Small. Hope yer don't get eaten by a humungous heffasaur or somethin'.'

I climbed the stairs to the doorway in the trunk and squeezed myself out onto the bough, scanning the sky through the mesh of branches for circling Pterodactyls. It was all clear.

I was sad leaving Spriggot behind, even though he was so bad-tempered. It would have been nice to have some company in this inhospitable place.

Someone's Watching! ◌◌

As I shinned down the tree, I heard a whirring noise and stopped, holding my breath and trying to work out where it was coming from. *I hope it's not those bloomin' vampire birds again*, I thought. But now I couldn't hear anything. I started down again and the whirring began once more. I stopped; the whirring stopped.

'Is that you, Spriggot?' I called out softly. 'You

don't have to creep along behind, you know.'
There was no reply. Then I froze as I spied a
glassy black eye staring at me from between
some branches. I moved my arm and
with a whirr, the eye swivelled to
follow it. What the heck was it?

Then, with a shock I
realized it wasn't an eye
at all. It was something
much weirder, and much
more worrying: the
glassy eye was a small,
whirring CCTV camera.
Something or someone
was watching my every
move.

It was a CCTV camera!

I quickly scurried to the
ground and began cautiously
picking my way through the forest. Now I could
see tiny cameras on almost every other tree,
moving as I moved, so I dived into a thicket of
large-leafed plants to try and get away from the
prying, electronic eyes.

I pushed on through, parting swathes of
hanging creepers and scratching my hands
on long, needle-like thorns. Then, as I cut

through a thick curtain of hanging foliage with my penknife, I stepped out into a clearing of springy, undulating grass, glowing ochre and green in the morning sunshine.

WHOOSH! I heard a sudden noise behind me and turned, terrified that the pterodactyl had returned. A winged beast was streaking towards me.

'Yikes!' I cried.

'There you are, Charlie. I thought I'd lost you,' buzzed Spriggot as the tiny man landed beside me in a flapping flurry of feathers on Darkness's back.

'Spriggot!' I cried with relief. 'What are you doing here?'

'I changed my mind about stayin' at home,' said the little man, jumping down from his feathery mount. 'I wasn't scared, mind. I just decided that it was time to move on and I thought you might be needin' some company, seein' as you're a stranger 'round here.'

'You're right,' I said. 'I would be glad of your company. I don't know where I'm going, though. I thought I'd head towards the cliffs and see if I can find a passage to the outside world.'

'Sounds good to me. This place has become

too crowded for my likin',' said the sprite. 'All right, Darkness, you can go now,' he added, patting the large raven on the shoulder. 'Thanks for the ride.'

'Caw,' the bird croaked loudly and looked quizzically at the sprite.

'Sure, if you want to,' said Spriggot. Then turning to me he said, 'She wants to come along with us, if that's OK with you.'

'The more the merrier,' I said, starting to feel as though I were in some sort of dark and sinister fairytale.

Signs Of Life

Darkness the raven flew up into the sky to act as look-out as Spriggot and I set off across the clearing towards the trees on the far side.

Although the little sprite was very small and very old, he was remarkably quick, leaping and darting from one tuft of grass to the next. It was almost like watching a flickering film as one minute he was standing beside me and a split second later he was five metres ahead, without seeming to move a muscle!

All the time he kept up a continuous buzz of grumbles and complaints. 'Why *would* somebody want to build a line of cliffs around this land? You used to be able to see all the way to the great North Ocean from the forest. Don't see no sense in it. No sense at all.'

'If you reckon the dinosaurs only appeared after the cliffs were built, I reckon they're there to keep the monsters in,' I said.

'Mmm, maybe,' said Spriggot a little reluctantly. 'But why?'

'I'm not sure,' I said. 'I don't know why there are CCTV cameras all over the forest, either.'

'CC whats?' asked Spriggot.

'Machines that record moving pictures through a glass eye,' I tried to explain.

'Ouch! You mean like this?' said Spriggot stubbing his toe and parting a clump of coarse grass to reveal another camera. 'I wondered what these whirrin' things were. I thought they were a new sort of insect.'

CWAWK! Suddenly, Darkness dropped from above with a terrified screech. Looking up at the patch of sky over our heads, I saw the eye and nose of the podgy-faced giant looming over us.

'Look, I *told* you there was a giant!' I cried, pointing up.

'I CAN SEE YOU, BOY,' the gargantuan face bellowed. 'YOU CAN'T AVOID YOUR FATE. YOU MUST PLAY THE GAME! HAHAHAHAH!'

Spriggot dived to the ground, shaking and shivering and trying to burrow under the long tufts of grass. 'Make it go away!' he buzzed in terror. Then, as quickly as it had appeared, the face flickered and then was gone.

'Let's not hang about,' I stammered, my knees knocking with fear. 'C'mon, Spriggot.' I grabbed his hand, yanking him to his feet and dragging him into a wide gap between the trees on the other side of the clearing.

'Hello, look!' I said, pointing down at our feet. 'It's the muddy tracks of a four-by-four. Someone's been driving a car through here. Maybe they'll be able to help us.'

A Puzzling Map

We followed the tracks, Darkness darting from branch to branch ahead of us. As we crept along the dim path, I spotted something lying on the muddy grass.

'Oh, wow! Take a look at this, Spriggot.' It was a scruffy, mud-spattered map of the enclosed jungle world.

Across the top of the page were some scuffed

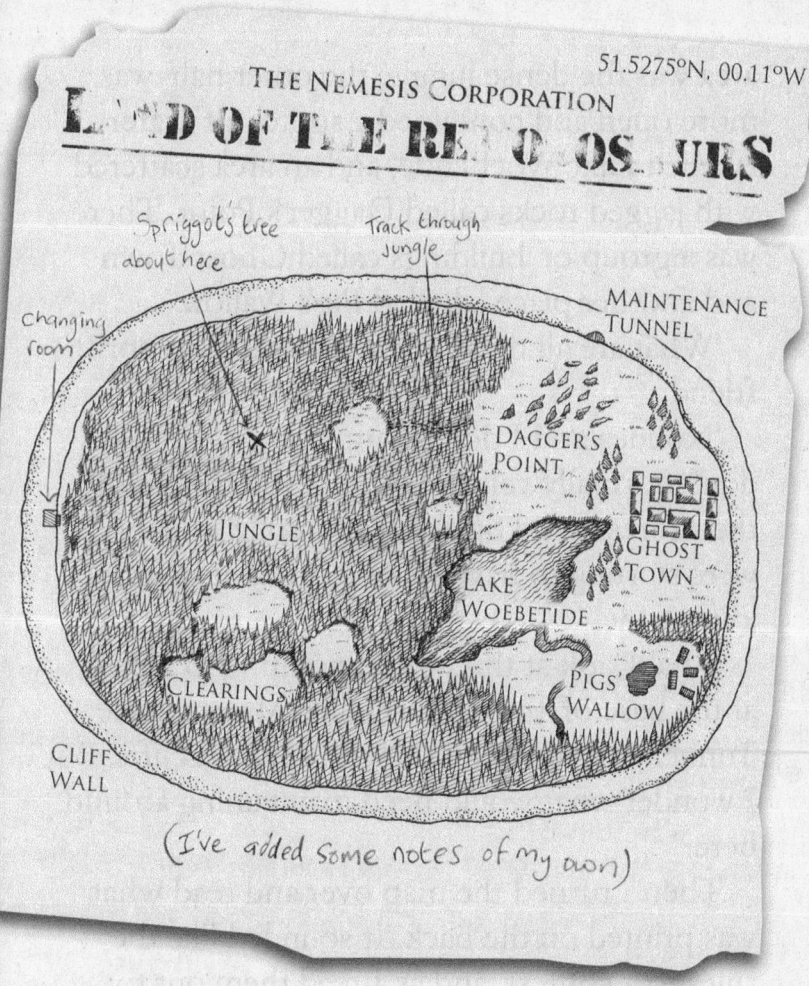

THE NEMESIS CORPORATION

L**D OF T**E RE**O**OS**URS

Spriggot's tree
about here

Track through
jungle

MAINTENANCE
TUNNEL

changing
room

DAGGER'S
POINT

JUNGLE

GHOST
TOWN

LAKE
WOEBETIDE

CLEARINGS

PIGS'
WALLOW

CLIFF
WALL

(I've added some notes of my own)

and scratched words: *The Nemesis Corporation, L**d Of T*e Re*o*os*urs,* and in the top corner were the coordinates 51.5275°N, 00.11°W. The map beneath showed the oval perimeter of the cliffs and the land inside them. One half of the area was the dense jungle; the other half was more open and contained a stretch of water labelled Lake Woebetide, and an area scattered with jagged rocks called Dagger's Point. There was a group of buildings called Ghost Town and another place labelled Pig's Wallow.

'What are all these places?' I asked my sprite friend.

'No idea and I don't want to know – sprites don't normally venture beyond the fringes of their forest,' said Spriggot grumpily, as if he were starting to have second thoughts about joining me.

'Aha! Look at this,' I said pointing to a place at the base of the cliffs labelled Maintenance Tunnel. 'Maybe that leads through the cliffs. But I wonder what would need maintaining around here?'

Then I turned the map over and read what was printed on the back. It sounded like the rules to a contest, and as I read them out to Spriggot I started to feel very uneasy:

'What's that all about?' I asked, suddenly feeling like a very small pawn in a much bigger game. A game that must have something to do with the giant in the sky.

'How do I know?' grumbled the sprite. 'Come on, the quicker we get out of here the better.'

A Beastly Battle

We hurried along the track between the trees, soon coming to the edge of the jungle, and stepped out onto a slope of tall grass. Spriggot was very nervous about leaving the confines of his wooded world so, to reassure him, I lifted him up to ride on my shoulders.

There were great, blade-shaped triangles of rock imbedded haphazardly in the ground before us, like discarded giant knives. Behind them rose the high retaining cliffs, looming over us and making me feel small, trapped and helpless.

'Those triangular rocks must be Dagger's Point,' I said, referring to the map. 'It's not far to the Maintenance Tunnel from here.'

Just then Darkness let out another warning '*CAW!*' and I dropped to my knees amongst the grasses.

The rocks at Dagger's Point

'What is it?' whispered Spriggot, leaping from my shoulders and hiding amongst the grassy tufts.

'I dunno, but Darkness must've seen something,' I whispered back. 'She . . .' But I was interrupted by a terrifying bellow as an

enormous, lumbering Triceratops raced from between two of the giant shards of granite. The ground rumbled and shook as if a traction engine were thundering down a cobbled street.

And after him sprinted a pair of snapping, spitting creatures.

They looked like Velociraptors, but were larger, about three metres long from nose to tail and as tall as a man. They hissed like snakes from crimson mouths as they approached the jumbo-sized Triceratops in a pincer movement.

(On checking my collector's cards later I discovered they were probably a dinosaur called Deinonychus, part of the same family as Velociraptors)

The Triceratops turned clumsily to meet them in combat, swinging its massive, horned head from side to side and trumpeting like an enraged elephant. Then as one raptor rushed at the Triceratops, snapping at its snout like a deranged dog, the other skirted behind the great beast. The Triceratops charged the one in front, hooked its horns under the raptor's belly and threw it high into the air. The Deinonychus somersaulted like a Jurassic gymnast and landed with a sickening thud on the stony ground.

The other raptor leaped onto the mighty Triceratops, sinking its teeth into the incensed dinosaur's back and making it leap and kick like a rodeo horse. As they charged and bucked in a fury of teeth and claws, the first raptor regained the few senses it possessed, scrambled to its feet and rushed at the foe. It struck at the Triceratops' throat and clung on for dear life as the monster snarled and shook and bucked and bellowed.

The snorting Triceratops put up a brave fight, but his smaller adversaries refused to let go. Gradually the beast was brought to the ground and, with a huge sigh, moved no more. I expected the Deinonychus to gorge themselves on the fallen Triceratops but, leaving it where it was, they trotted right past us and with loud snorting hisses headed off towards the forest. I let out my breath; I'd been holding it the whole time, both fascinated and appalled by the battle.

A Remotosaur

'Steamin' great cowpats!' gasped Spriggot, his whole body shaking and his voice buzzing like a trapped fly. 'We've got to get out of here *now*, Charlie.'

'Too right,' I said in a wobbly voice, fear-fuelled adrenalin coursing through my veins. 'Come on, but be careful. If those things spot us, we're dead meat – they could outrun a cheetah.'

Spriggot and I got cautiously to our feet and in a crouching run made our way towards the dagger-like stones. We had to pass right by the gigantic body of the fallen Triceratops and, although I knew it was a dangerous thing to do, I *had* to go and investigate. It's not often you get the chance of walking up to a real dinosaur, dead *or* alive.

'You sure it's dead?' Spriggot asked nervously as we approached. I stretched out my hand and gently poked the creature's stomach. It didn't move. I poked it harder, and when there was still no response I breathed more easily and walked around to look at the dinosaur's head. It was the size of a small car, covered with olive green skin as wrinkly as a rhino's, and had a long muzzle that curved into a pointed, beak-like mouth. Three long horns

I gave it a prod

grew from its forehead and nose and a big, bony, protective plate fanned out over its neck.

'Wow, this is awesome,' I whispered. I'd never seen anything so amazing. Then I noticed a long gash in the creature's throat and winced. *That looks really painful*, I thought. *So, how come there's no blood?* I crouched down and crawled under the dino's chin for a closer look.

'What the heck are you doin'?' buzzed Spriggot. 'This ain't no time to play silly beggars! Come on, let's go.'

'Just a tick,' I said. 'I want to have a look . . . well, I never!'

'Well you never what?' snapped Spriggot, getting impatient.

'I never would've believed it,' I said, folding back a flap of skin to reveal a severed cord in the animal's throat – a cord of frayed copper wiring! I shone my torch inside and saw a whole mess of wrecked electrics, hydraulics and mechanics. 'This isn't a real dinosaur – it's a robot! What's going on, Spriggot?'

'Beats me,' said the little man, crossing his arms and tapping his foot. 'I don't care if they're flesh and blood or steel and oil. They're big, scary and deadly and hangin' around here is askin' fer trouble. Now are you ready?'

'In a mo,' I said, pulling the map from my pocket.

'Oh, dollopin' doodahs, what now?' Spriggot got down on his hands and knees and crawled beside me.

'Yeah, I thought so, look!' I cried, holding out the map. 'It says *The Nemesis Corporation, Land of the Remotosaurs*. These things are remote-controlled dinosaurs. But what is The Nemesis Corporation?' Just then I felt a tug at my holster as someone smoothly removed my ray gun. At the same time, Spriggot let out a cry.

'That would be *me*,' said a menacing voice.

Oh yikes!

Nemesis Gamer

I crawled from below the Triceratops' chin and found myself staring into the pudgy face of the giant in the sky. Except he wasn't a giant any more but a short, tubby man in a long black coat, his eyes hidden behind a pair of dark glasses. He leaned against a yellow vehicle that had a ray gun rifle mounted on its cab.

I'm Nemesis Gamer

'*I'm* Nemesis Gamer,' hissed the man with a wheezing voice as his tongue darted like a snake from between thin, colourless lips. He had a bald head and a long ponytail tied with a thin black ribbon. Shiny black boots came up to the knees of his black jeans and he had my ray gun in one podgy hand pointed straight at me. In the other he held a swearing and kicking Spriggot by the leg.

'Where's Darkness?' the sprite squeaked, upside-down.

'Your feathered look-out? Zapped! She has cawed her last caw, I'm afraid, *sss-sss-sss*,' said the man with a horrid, hissing chuckle, pointing to where our dear faithful friend lay crumpled and motionless on the ground.

'You fiend!' yelled Spriggot, wriggling and kicking. 'You'll pay for that!'

'I don't think so. Now, be quiet!' Gamer snapped in his soft, menacing voice, shaking the struggling sprite.

'You were a giant,' I said stupidly. 'I saw you up in the sky!'

'Gave you a fright, did I?' the man said with a hoarse whisper. 'It was only my image projected on the glass roof. Quite effective though, isn't it? *Sss-sss-sss.*'

'You might have scared me as a giant, but yɔ d-don't scare me now,' I lied, trying to sound brave.

'Oh, don't go thinking that I'm not to be feared, just because I'm a little shorter than you imagined,' said Gamer coldly. 'I am completely and utterly ruthless.'

I believed him. Although he looked like an ordinary, pudgy and rather scruffy little man, Nemesis Gamer was clearly a thoroughly nasty piece of work.

'Now tell me who you are and how you got into my game,' he hissed.

'I don't know what you're on about,' I said, confused.

'*This!*' said the man, waving the ray gun about to indicate the whole area. 'This is my Remotosaur Gaming Stadium and you are trespassing, you interloping insect. I repeat, who are you and what are you doing here?'

'My name is Charlie Small and I ended up here by accident. If you can show me how to get out, I'll gladly be on my way,' I said.

'Ha! That's not going to happen, Charlie Small, *sss-sss-sss.* You're staying here, you snivelling pest.'

'You can't leave me here!' I cried. 'I might be ripped apart by a dinosaur.'

'That's what happens to trespassers,' said Nemesis. 'I'll be taking this wriggling thing with me, though. What is it?'

'I *can* talk, yer know,' yelled a furious Spriggot, flailing about upside down. 'I'm a forest sprite.'

'A sprite? Wow! I thought they only existed in kids' fairytales,' Gamer said. 'There'll be money to be made from you, little feller, *sss-sss-sss*. How many more sprites live in the forest?'

'I'm the only one,' growled Spriggot, landing a kick to the man's podgy gut. 'We ain't very sociable!'

'Ooof!' gasped Gamer. 'Right you little pest, you asked for it.' He threw the forest sprite through the open window into the truck's passenger seat, got in himself and turned the key in the ignition. An electric engine hummed quietly into life.

'So long, Charlie Small,' grinned Nemesis Gamer, showing an uneven line of small, khaki-coloured teeth. 'Good luck with the Remotosaurs. If you prove a popular target, I might well catch me some more kids to put in here. They might be even better sport than the Pig Troopers.' He gave a final sneer as he released the brakes and shot off, the car's wheels spinning and throwing up great clods of grassy peat in its wake.

'Charlie!' I heard Spriggot cry.

'Come back. Let him go, you great oaf,' I yelled, my brain reeling in confusion. Game stadium; targets; Pig Troopers – what *was* this terrible place I had stumbled into?

Run And Hide

I darted after the truck as it wove its way through the rocks of Dagger's Point, but I was soon left behind. I could only watch as the truck disappeared inside the Maintenance Tunnel a hundred metres away, and heavy doors closed behind it.

A few seconds later I arrived at the tall, steel doors in the cliff. I grabbed the edge of one and tried to open it, but it was futile – they were firmly bolted from the inside. There wasn't even a keyhole that I could pick.

'Darn it!' I yelled and kicked the doors until they boomed and shook. 'Let me out of here, you whispering weasel!' It was the wrong thing to do – it must have sounded like a dino's dinner gong. As the booming echoes died away, a low pulsating growl sounded from behind me. Emerging from the nearby rocks of Dagger's Point was a ferocious, snarling Tyrannosaurus Rex!

'It's not real,' I told myself. 'It's only a machine!' But that didn't help at all. I knew that if these things were half as sophisticated as one of my pal Jakeman's mechanical inventions, they would be a formidable foe. Taller than a giraffe, it towered over me and started edging forwards, snapping its ginormous jaws.

I reached for my ray gun, but of course the holster was empty.

'Drat that man,' I yelled and felt inside my rucksack for my lasso – only to remember it had been shredded by a space balloon's propellor. There was nothing in there to help me, and I cursed myself for not restocking my explorer's kit. Then I remembered a bit of advice I'd read in one of my adventure books. *If you can't fight – run! You might live to fight another day.*

It was good advice and I pelted towards the largest rock sticking from the ground. As I dived behind the stone, the T-Rex lunged forward; its jaws closed on thin air with a crash and it gave a mighty grunt of frustration.

I peeped over the top of the stone. The T-Rex seemed to have lost me for a moment and was looking gormlessly about with its tiny, blank eyes. I started to spot the nuts and bolts that hinged the mechanical dinosaur's jaws and legs. Some of its rubberized skin was frayed and worn, like the fabric of an old sofa – and then I saw something else I hadn't noticed before. Set into the dinosaur's belly was a small, flickering screen – on the screen was the image of a boy.

What's that in aid of? I wondered. Then I

(See my journal Planet of The Geeks!)

noticed the boy was holding a control pad, staring straight at me and feverishly flicking the buttons with his thumbs. As he did so the monstrous robot lurched towards me. The boy grinned and stabbed at the pad again. The T-Rex's jaws opened in a rictus grin, and it suddenly dawned on me – *the boy was controlling the dinosaur!*

I stepped out from my hiding place, waving my arms and shouting. 'Stop! I'm a real boy! This is not a game!'

I thought the boy saw me but I don't think he could hear, because the next second he jabbed a button and the dinosaur pounced.

There was an image of a boy on a monitor

Flippin' heck, I thought as the T-Rex raised its colossal head and brought it thundering down towards me. I rolled away just in time as the stone behind me shattered into a thousand fragments. The dino lifted its head to roar at the sky as I crouched shivering behind another slab. I held my breath and listened as the creature looked for me, its great clawed feet thumping on the ground, and rocks crashing down as it pushed them over with its bullet head.

Everything went quiet but I stayed where I was, not daring to make a sound. I waited for ages until I was sure the creature had gone in search of other prey. Then I cautiously raised my head to check. The T-Rex was not there. Letting out a huge sigh of relief, I stood up.

RARRR! An ear-thumping bellow exploded to my left and the T-Rex emerged from its hiding place behind a large standing stone and rushed towards me, its crimson mouth wide open and its scythe-like teeth glinting in the sunshine. On the screen, the boy was frowning with concentration, stabbing at the buttons as a nasty sneer curled his lip.

I tried to run, but the creature had blocked my only escape route and was towering over me.

'WOOAARR!' T-Rex bellowed again. It flourished its stubby clawed arms and whipped its great tail through the air, knocking over rocks like rows of dominos. As it pounced, the creature's muzzle caught me a crushing blow on the head and I collapsed to the ground, stunned. (Thank goodness for my helmet, or my head would have cracked open like a boiled egg!) In the confusion I remember seeing a movement from the corner of my eye. The next moment a bolt of red light shot through the air, hitting the T-Rex on its shoulder. Sparks fizzed and crackled as the dinosaur backed away, nursing a smoking wound and baring its fangs at its new enemy. Another beam of red light hit it and this time the dinosaur took to its heels and ran. The next moment someone was standing over me.

'Are you all right?' asked a thick, guttural voice.

'Yeah, I think so,' I replied, raising my spinning head to see a fuzzy figure dressed in the same uniform as mine. My eyes cleared for a moment and I gasped – it was a long-snouted, muddy and bristled bush pig who looked like he was wearing clothes. *A pig?* I thought. *In a uniform?* Then I passed out.

Pig Paddlers

When I came to, I was lying in a flat-bottomed canoe. There was a strong farmyard whiff in the air and when I looked around I saw two pigs paddling and a third sitting on a plank seat near my head, looking out from the prow like a galleon's figurehead.

'What's going on? Let me out of here,' I cried in a panic, fearing that I was being kidnapped. I tried to sit up but my head was throbbing with pain and I collapsed back down into the bottom of the boat.

'Whoa! Calm *grunt* down! We're not going to hurt you – we just rescued you from the jaws of a T-Rex for *grunt* goodness sakes!' snorted the pig at the front of the canoe. 'Now lie back and rest for a bit.'

I stared up at my rescuers. They had long, wide snouts with two bulging tusks, small piercing eyes and short, stumpy legs. Even more bizarrely, the three pigs were wearing exactly the same uniform as me – black tops with a reinforced chest guard and a yellow lightning

bolt logo – though theirs were extremely muddy. They also had ray guns and the same helmet as me, and I now realized why it was such a strange shape – it was designed for a pig's head, not a boy's! And no wonder the trousers had been much too short for me – they only had little short legs!

I raised myself onto my elbows and peered over the side. We were in the middle of Lake Woebetide, speeding along over choppy little waves whipped up by a strong breeze.

'Who are you and where are you taking me?' I asked.

'*Grunt.* We're the *snort* Pig Troopers,' said the main pig at the prow, turning his long, hairy face and looking down at me with interest. 'Don't *snort* worry. We're taking you back to our wallow where we can dress that wound *grunt* on your head. *Weeh-weeh!* You've got quite a nasty bump there *grunt*!' And the pig reached down and gently brushed back the hair from my forehead with a little orange, bristly hand.

'Are we safe out here on the lake?' I asked, as the water got rougher. Now the canoe was being lifted from the surface by the breakers and dropped with a bone-juddering slap.

'Safe as *snort* houses, young man,' smiled the boar. 'As long as we don't bump into the . . . *Whoa*!'

At that moment the waters in front of us parted in an explosion of spray, and something long and smooth, black and horned burst from the depths below.

'. . . *Sea serpent*!' cried the pig as our canoe was lifted on the reptile's snaking back, then went sliding off and dropped nose first into the swirling foam.

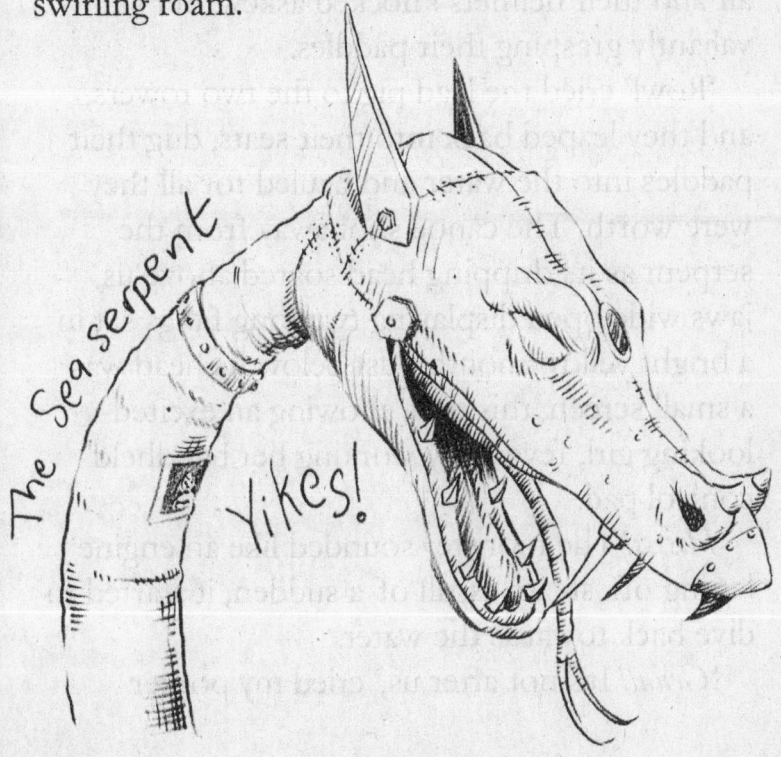

The Sea serpent

Yikes!

We disappeared into the lake like an arrow. Bubbles cascaded about us and water pounded in my ears. Down and down we streaked – then *whoosh*! We began to rise like a cork, breaking the surface, shooting into the air and dropping right side up onto the lake.

I was still lying on the bottom of the canoe, holding on to one of the plank seats for all I was worth. The pigs were scattered about, upside down with their trotters thrashing in the air and their helmets knocked askew, but still valiantly grasping their paddles.

'Row!' cried the lead pig to the two rowers, and they leaped back into their seats, dug their paddles into the water and hauled for all they were worth. The canoe shot away from the serpent as its dripping head soared above us, jaws wide open displaying two long fangs set in a bright yellow mouth. Just below its head was a small screen, this time showing an excited-looking girl, feverishly working her handheld control pad.

Hissss! The monster sounded like an engine letting off steam as, all of a sudden, it started to dive back towards the water.

'*Grunt!* It's not after us,' cried my porker

friend. 'It's after something under the suface. *Grunt snort weeh!*'

With hardly a splash the serpent's head entered the lake, its thick, tubular body following in a continuous glide. Suddenly, just up ahead, a large scallop-finned fish leaped high out of the water in a desperate bid to escape.

'He's for it,' said the pig.

A fish leaped out of the water!

'Doesn't stand *grunt* a chance,' agreed one of the rowers – and they were right. As the wide-mouthed guppy arced back towards the lake, the serpent's head rose just behind and with a *snap!* the fish was gone.

'That could have been us!' I cried. 'That fish was as big as this canoe.' Before the pigs had a chance to reply, the tail of the serpent whipped up from below as the creature aimed its head for the depths of the lake and dived. The tail flipped our boat from the water and sent it spinning and flipping through the air.

We landed with an almighty splash and went scudding across the water like a skimming pebble, coming to a juddering halt on a muddy bank.

'*Yeehah!*' I yelled, exhilarated by the ride. 'That was better than the log flume at a theme park!'

Out Cold!

The pigs immediately jumped from the canoe and hauled it further up the shore and into the shelter of some low bushes. They looked very comical with their stout, barrel bodies as they trotted daintily about on short little legs, snuffling and heaving and burping as they struggled with the long craft.

I clambered from the boat and followed them through some scrub onto a dusty path.

'Right young man *oink*,' grunted the lead pig. He only came up to my waist and peered up at me with small, round eyes. 'Now we're out of trouble, I think we can introduce ourselves. My name is Hock and I'm the leader of the Pig Troopers. These are two of my squad *weeh*.'

'Pleased to meet you *grunt* I'm sure,' said one of the pig paddlers. 'I'm Sage.' He was a little shorter than Hock, his shoulders were much narrower and his bristles a paler colour.

'And I'm Penelope,' said the other. She didn't have any tusks at all and was as round as a Christmas pudding!

'My name is Charlie Small. I'm an eight-year-old adventurer who's lived for four hundred years and I'm very, very confused,' I said.

I'm Penelope

'That'll be *burp* the bump on your head making you dizzy,' said Hock. 'Let's get you back to camp.'

'No, I'm confused about all *this*,' I said, waving my arms in the air. 'The Remotosaurs; this stadium; Nemesis Gamer; *you*. It's all such a jumble.' Then the bump on my head started to throb and pound and I crumpled to the floor.

'Don't *grunt* move, Charlie. We'll *burp* carry you the rest of the way,' said Hock. 'Just lie *weeh* easy.'

The bump on my head started to throb!

I watched through swimming eyes as the pigs snapped branches from the bushes. They pulled off some of the huge leaves and tied them between two branches with fibrous reeds, to act as a stretcher. Then they carefully lifted me onto it, picked it up and set off at a trot.

I must have drifted into a deep sleep, because I don't remember anything about the journey. When I woke up it was the middle of the night. I was in a long, corrugated iron hut in the shape of a half cylinder. One end was open to the night air and I could see a fire glowing in the dark outside, spitting little orange sparks into the sky. I was lying on a pile of straw, covered with a soft blanket of dried lichen and surrounded by snoring, grunting and incredibly smelly pigs. I was very comfy and with a smile closed my eyes and drifted back to sleep.

A Week In Bed

When I woke again it was late in the morning. I sat up slowly; my head was still tender but it wasn't thumping any more. Penelope was sitting beside me and beamed when she saw me wake up.

'*Weeh* good morning, Charlie,' she said. 'Just stay where you are. I'll *grunt* go and get Hock.'

A few minutes later she returned with the pig leader. They looked just like clockwork toys as their short, tubby legs hurried them along.

'Ah, good to see you awake, Charlie. Feeling any better?' he grunted.

'Yeah, much better thanks,' I replied. 'I think

I'll get up now, I should be on my way.'

'On your way *grunt* where?' asked the pig.

'I've got to rescue Spriggot and find a way out of here,' I explained.

'What's a Spriggot?' grunted the boar.

'He's a sprite I met in the forest,' I said.

'A *sprite*? Mmm, I think that bump on the head is still affecting you,' snorted Hock.

'No, honest! Nemesis Gamer took him,' I said.

'You'd better tell me just what's been going *grunt* on!' said Hock.

So I told him how I'd left home on my raft so long ago, and what happened after I found myself in the dinosaur kingdom. 'So you see I've got to go. Spriggot's in trouble and my mum is expecting me home in time for tea. I've already been gone four hundred years and I don't want to be late!'

'That's one incredible *snort* story,' said the astounded pig. 'But you must rest *grunt*. You need to build your strength up. You've been out cold for a week.'

'*A week* – you're kidding!' I exclaimed.

Hock shook his head. 'No, really,' he said. 'Now do as you're told and let us take care of you. Are you hungry?'

I nodded. 'Famished,' I said.

'Penelope will bring you something,' he said, his bristly snout wrinkling into a smile. 'Rest, and I'll come back and see you when you're feeling stronger.'

So, for the second time in the land of the Remotosaurs I have found myself confined to a sickbed! Over the last two days, Penelope the pig has waited on me hand and foot. She has brought me bowls of coarse, cold porridge with raw brussel sprouts floating in it, mugs of warm, muddy-tasting tea, and ointment to rub into the bruise on my forehead.

I am very cosy snuggled amongst the straw in the corrugated hut. It sleeps about twenty pigs if we all squash up together, and there is always one of them coming or going and stopping for a chat. They are very friendly, but don't tell me much. If I ask them about the Remotosaurs or Nemesis Gamer, they just say that Hock will tell me all I need to know when I am better.

In the evenings everyone gathers around

the campfire to eat, and there's such a hubbub of chatting and squealing and grunting I'm surprised they can hear themselves speak. Some of the pigs bring their meal up to the hut and sit with me while I eat. As you would expect, their table manners leave a lot to be desired; they talk with their mouths full and cheer loudly if someone lets out a particularly fruity belch!

BURP!

During the day I've been writing up this journal and have checked all the stuff in my explorer kit. This is what it contains at the moment:

1) My multi-tooled penknife
2) A ball of string (getting smaller all the time!)
3) A feather from Octavia Moon, the giant owl that flew me to the frozen North

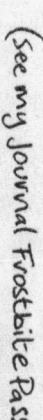

(see my Journal Frostbite Pass)

4) A telescope
5) A scarf (complete with bullet holes!)
6) An old railway ticket
7) This journal
8) A pack of wild animal collector's cards (full of amazing animal facts, but fails to mention that Vampire Birds are poisonous!)
9) A glue pen to stick things in my notebook
10) A glass eye from my brave steam-powered rhinoceros friend
11) The compass and torch I found on the sun-bleached skeleton of a lost explorer
12) The tooth of a monstrous megashark (makes a handy saw)
13) A magnifying glass (for starting fires etc)
14) A radio
15) My mobile phone with wind-up charger (to speak to Mum)
16) The (broken) skull of a Barbarous Bat
17) A bundle of maps and diagrams collected on my adventures
18) A bag of marbles
19) A battered water bottle
20) A plastic lemon full of lemon juice (nearly empty now!)

21) The bony finger of an animated skeleton (handy for picking locks)

Around my neck I still wear the great diamond that Chief Sitting Pretty awarded me for helping save his son from the two-headed vulture, Mapwai.

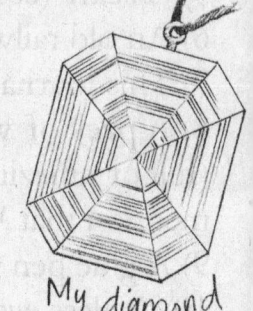

My diamond

I'm feeling a bit better now. My head still has a lump as big as an egg, but I need to find out what's going on in this crazy place! I need to make plans. So tomorrow I'm going to get up – I'm really looking forward to it, as Penelope said I could have a bath in the morning, and I *really* need one. I haven't had a good wash for weeks!

The Pigs' Wallow

The sun was streaming through the glass roof high above our heads when I finally woke up and got out of bed. At last I was well again! As I stepped gingerly out of the hut, I saw that there were three others close to the one I was sleeping in, all the same shape and size. The air around them was thick with a strong piggy smell. Behind the huts was a semicircle of trees that formed a small spinney. A crowd of snorting piglets played noisily amongst them.

Beyond the campfire, about ten metres in front of the huts, was a wide bowl-shaped depression in the ground and at the bottom was a pond of thick, black glutinous mud. I looked a bit closer and saw that Penelope, Sage, Hock and a very tubby porker called Crackling were rolling around in the mire, splashing and squealing with piggy delight!

'Come on, Charlie, dive in!' cried Crackling, rolling around joyfully.

'Um, I'd love to but I'm going to have a bath this morning,' I said.

'This *is* our bath *oink* silly,' grunted Penelope. 'Surely you know pigs wallow in mud baths?'

'It's great for the complexion!' cried Sage, rubbing great handfuls of black, foul-smelling sludge into his face.

'It's wonderful,' snorted Hock. 'What's keeping you *burp,* Charlie?'

'Oh well,' I sighed. 'If you can't beat 'em!'

Stripping to my shorts I took a run-up, leaping into the wallow and landing with a loud *kersplat!*, sending a great dollop of mud into the air, splattering down on my piggy friends.

'*Weeeh!*' cried the pigs. 'Way to go, Charlie!'

I rolled around in the warm, smelly bog, coating my face and hands and hair. The pigs were right – it was wonderful!

The Game Explained

Yes, sah!

Clambering out, we lay on the bank letting the mud dry to a crust on our skin. Then, after pulling on our uniforms, we ate a breakfast of lightly fried turnip crisps and a stodgy bread with sugar beet spread. Afterwards, Hock briefed a small troop of pigs who saluted him smartly and went scurrying away through the spinney towards the lake.

'Where are they going?' I asked Hock, rubbing great flakes of mud from my hair.

'To do a recce of the area. We've got to keep the Remotosaurs away from our wallow. If they attacked us here we wouldn't stand a chance. As it is we're losing at least one trooper a week,' he replied.

'Losing?' I asked. 'You don't mean . . .'

'They are either swallowed whole by a mechanical T-Rex, or taken off by a robotic pterodactyl,' said Hock, shaking his head. 'Not a happy ending. And they are out of the game.'

'That's terrible,' I said. 'But what do you mean by "out of the game"?'

'The game, Charlie. This whole thing is one big game devised by *grunt* Nemesis Gamer.' said Hock.

I couldn't believe my ears. A game?

Hock continued: 'I'll try to explain as simply as I can. Nemesis Gamer built metal cliffs around an old jungle to create his gaming stadium and filled it with mechanical, remote-controlled dinosaurs of his own invention.

Then he travelled to my homeland, Swinedon, captured a herd of pigs and *weeh* brought us here. He said he needed a tribe of real *grunt* fighters to take on the remote-controlled dinosaurs. He made us put on these uniforms and released us into the stadium.'

'So who are the children I've seen on the Remotosaurs' built-in monitors?' I interrupted. 'Are they Nemesis Gamer's sidekicks?'

'No, that's the dreadful thing about it, Charlie. They are normal kids; children just like you, up in their bedrooms or in front of the telly playing on their gaming stations. It's *them* who are controlling the rampaging Remotosaurs,' grunted Hock.

'That's terrible. How could anyone send a mechanical dinosaur careering after a harmless bush pig?' I protested.

'It's not their fault – it's just a game to them. A fast, exciting shoot-em-up game,' said the boar, shaking his head. 'Nemesis Gamer has developed some computer software *weeh* and released it as a game called *Land of the Remotosaurs*. Everyone who's bought a copy is astounded by the quality of the *grunt* graphics, not knowing they are actually seeing real, live images sent from hidden cameras all over this ginormous gaming stadium. The kids don't know the dinosaurs they control are ten metre-long machines, or the little pigs they chase are squeaking, grunting, intelligent beings; not computer-generated images, but real pork and blood!' The hairy hog looked as if he was going to explode with outrage.

'This is terrible!' I exclaimed. 'We've got to stop Gamer before we're all annihilated. I've got to rescue poor little Spriggot – and, oh my goodness, Nemesis said he was going to put some kids in here to fight the Remotosaurs; I've got to put an end to this game before he has the chance!'

Making Plans

'Come with me,' said Hock, and led me through the spinney of young trees to where we could see the massive metal cliffs on the other side of the stadium.

'Do you *oink* see where the cliffs bulge up to their highest?' he asked, pointing along the escarpment. 'I think that's where Nemesis *grunt* Gamer has his control centre. You can see some windows, and occasionally I've noticed the sun reflecting off something inside, as if *weeh* he's scanning the stadium with binoculars.'

I took the telescope from my rucksack and swept it over the top of the cliff, where it joined the glass roof. There were four windows set into a curved section of cliff, looking out over the whole stadium. A plan started to form in my mind. 'If I could get in there without Gamer

There were some windows at the top of the cliff

knowing, I might be able to make my way to the maintenance tunnel doors, open them from the inside and let your troops in. Then we could smash the controls to stop the Remotosaurs.'

'That would be great *grunt* Charlie – but it's a harder climb than you might think. Look,' said Hock, pointing further down the cliff face.

I slowly lowered the telescope, studying the rough metal cliff. When it got to a certain level the cliff became as smooth as a slide, all the way to the ground, making it impossible to climb. Nemesis Gamer had ensured that none of his captors could reach his hideout.

'It's virtually unscaleable,' grunted Hock. 'I've tried climbing it, but there are no footholds and my trotters just scrabble about on the shiny surface.'

I aimed the telescope to where the cliffs met the ground. There were a group of thin pine trees near the base. 'Mmm, that might work,' I said.

'What *grunt,* Charlie?' asked Hock.

'Just an idea,' I said. 'Hello, what are those buildings?'

'Oh, that's Ghost Town,' snorted the boar. 'It's a group of deserted buildings – another area for gamers to play in. There are often Remotosaurs prowling around the area, stalking each other. We keep well away from it.'

'Well, we're going to have to get past if we've got any chance of climbing to Nemesis Gamer's lair,' I said. 'Monsters or no monsters, I need to get to those pine trees. We'll need four strong pigs; a long length of creeper and a sharp axe.'

I explained the rest of my plan to Hock and, although he clearly thought I was barmy, he agreed we should try it. But I have no idea what will happen if I manage to get into Gamer's lair – ah well, I'll worry about all that when I get there. In the meantime I've got to get into training and build my strength up. I need to be as fit as a fiddle.

The Next Day

5 press-ups; 5 sit-ups; half a kilometre jog.

The Day After That

10 press-ups; 10 sit-ups; three-quarters of a kilometre jog.

The Following Day

25 press-ups; 25 sit-ups; one-and-a-half kilometre jog – I'm feeling on top form again now. My head is better, I've had a good rest, done some training and been eating really well.

Over the last few days Hock has led a squad of pigs out of camp to draw the Remotosaurs away from our wallow. There has been some ferocious fighting, as unwitting gamers at home on their computers sent the dinosaurs in to do battle with the poor pig troopers. No casualties though!

While Hock was out on patrol, I stayed at the wallow with the rest of the pigs. I've got to know them really well over the last few days, from the littlest piglet to the oldest, bewhiskered sow, and they are all friendly, brave, funny . . .

and oh, so smelly! Each evening, when Hock returns from his patrol, we sit and go over our plan.

Now it's time for bed – it's still early but I want to get a good night's sleep, because tomorrow I'm going to try to break into Nemesis Gamer's cliff-top lair! It's going to be difficult and dangerous, but I've got to give it a go if I want to save Spriggot and end Nemesis Gamer's deadly computer game.

I've finished writing up my journal, the pigs are snoring all around me and the peaty fire outside is filling the air with a rich, earthy perfume, making my eyelids heavy. I'll write more when I can. Goodnight.

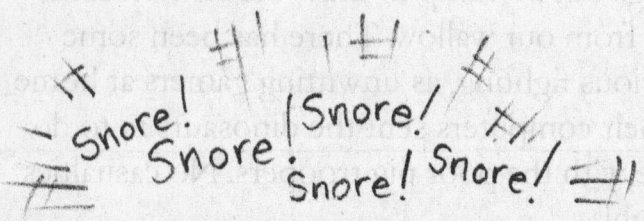

Note to self: remember to fill one of the small plastic bags I use for collecting samples with gloopy mud from the pigs' wallow.

Ghost Town!

The next morning, I checked that we had all the things I needed for my plan, and soon Hock, Sage, Penelope, Crackling and me, were heading towards Ghost Town. The pigs' legs moved in a blur as they hurried to keep up with me, grunting and snorting with effort. After twenty minutes of trekking, sneaking along behind bushes to avoid prowling Remotosaurs, we arrived at our destination.

On the outskirts of Ghost Town, Hock raised his hand, signalling for us to hunker down. We waited in silence, scanning the broken-down buildings ahead.

'It all seems *snort* quiet,' said Hock in a hoarse whisper. 'Come on, but keep your eyes peeled and have your ray guns at the ready.'

We hurried forward in a crouching run and I pulled my newly-given ray gun from its holster and curled my finger around the trigger.

We flattened ourselves against the wall of the first building and moved quietly along to the corner. Hock peeped around the edge.

'All clear,' he said and we scuttled down a

narrow side alley. We stopped at the end and again Hock checked the scene.

'OK, nothing here,' he said and we stepped out into the empty main street.

Ghost town!

It reminded me of Trouble, the cowboy town where I'd robbed a bank with the Daredevil Desperados of Destiny. The low buildings were brick and timber constructions with a covered sidewalk down both sides of the street. The windows were cracked and broken and litter blew noisily across the dusty road. As the wind gusted down the deserted alleys, it made a mournful whine that sounded horribly spooky.

'No wonder it's called Ghost Town,' I said. 'Come on, let's get a move on.'

As we turned to head towards the cliffs, a *huge* Deinonychus stepped out from behind a building and blocked the end of the street. It was much bigger than the mechanical creatures that had attacked the Triceratops, and looked a lot like a Tyranosaurus Rex. Its rubberized skin was brown and knobbly; it had a massive pair of jaws lined with glistening steel teeth, claws like cutlasses and was almost as high as the buildings.

'Uh oh,' I said, turning around. 'Let's go this way.'

Another Deinonychus appeared at the other end of the street. With idiotic leers the two dinosaurs licked their scaly lips with enormous pink rubber tongues and then, at exactly the same time and without a roar of warning, they charged from either end, their mechanical legs pumping like pistons.

Two of the pigs dropped to their knees, aimed their ray guns and fired. Thin beams of red light shot down the street, but the creatures sidestepped the rays and kept on coming. The pigs fired again. One Deinonychus was caught on the leg. It stumbled as a plume of smoke rose from a tear in its fabric skin, but it ploughed straight on, its thin snout snapping and snarling.

'Into the buildings!' cried Hock and we scattered, three to one side of the street and two to the other.

I followed Hock and Penelope up some stairs and over to the window of the front room. We glanced out, careful not to be seen. The two Deinonychus were prowling down the opposite side of the street, peering in at the first floor windows and snapping their jaws. All of a sudden, one darted its head through an empty window and brought out a struggling pig.

'It's got Sage,' cried Penelope. '*Weeh!*'

A shower of beams hit the raptor, knocking it sideways, but it regained its footing and with a flip of its neck threw Sage into the air, opened its jaws and swallowed the poor little mite whole.

'You devil!' I yelled from the window and fired my ray gun again and again at the beast, but it had no effect. The machines were as large and heavy as bulldozers and were not going to be stopped easily.

'Aim for the head!' cried Hock. 'See that small black disc between its eyes? Knock that out and the remote control will stop working!' He fired, but the dinosaur anticipated his move and ducked. 'Whoever is controlling this beast is a brilliant gamer,' snorted the boar and fired again.

Zap! This time his beam hit the disc and the Deinonychus faltered.

Zap! I fired and hit the spot.

Zap, zap, zap! Hock, Penelope and I all fired at once and with a small burst of flame the radar panel burnt out and the dinosaur stopped mid-stride. It stood still like a statue for just a moment, then slowly and with a terrible crash toppled to the ground.

'One down, one to *grunt* go,' said Hock, grimly. 'No one eats one of my pals and gets away with it. *Snort!*'

Pig Rescue

The other dinosaur was being bombarded by shots from Crackling, the only remaining pig over the road. He ran from one window to another, firing all the time, and the raptor didn't know which way to turn. It roamed back and forth, roaring and smashing at the wooden walls.

Its head was level with the windows and in sudden frustration it clamped its jaws around the sill and ripped a great section out of the wall. Crackling backed against the far side of the room as the dino tried desperately to reach him. We fired and fired, but because it had its back to us, we couldn't see the receiver disc on its forehead.

'Wait here,' I said to my piggy comrades. 'I'm going to try and attract its attention. When you get a clear shot, bring it down.'

I jumped from the window onto the roof above the sidewalk and then slid down an upright support onto the road.

'What *weeh* are you doing, Charlie?' squealed Hock. 'Come back and that's *grunt* an order!' But I was already halfway across the street.

'Get ready,' I shouted at my pals as I ran up behind the raptor. I grabbed its huge tail under an arm and tugged for all I was worth. The dinosaur didn't feel a thing! As it stuck its head into the room above to make another grab for Crackling, it swung its tail and I was thrown down the road landing next to the dinosaur we had already felled.

As I got to my feet, I heard a strange thumping coming from its chest. I backed away, wondering what it could be. Was the beast still functioning? I didn't have time to hang around though, and raced back to the rampaging raptor, waving my arms and yelling at the top of my voice.

This time the dopey dinosaur noticed me, and with a leer it turned and approached on its great, scaly legs like some sort of high-stepping giant bird. I slowly walked backwards down the road, watching the dinosaur for any sudden movements, until I had my back to the window where my pals were hiding. Then, as the beast suddenly charged I caught sight of the screen in its chest and gasped in disbelief. I couldn't believe it! Looking out was my best friend Philly! She was obviously playing *Land of the Remotosaurs* on her computer at home (or wherever she was)!

'Philly, STOP!' I yelled, waving my arms like crazy as she raced the beast towards me like an express train. 'STOP!' I cried again, jumping up and down like a loon. 'It's me, Charlie Small!'

All of a sudden Philly's face looked closer and her mouth fell open and straightaway the

great beast skidded to a halt; then Philly started mouthing something, but I couldn't understand what on earth she was trying to say.

It was Philly!

'I'm stuck in a life-size gaming station,' I yelled, taking the crumpled map out of my pocket and holding it up to the screen. 'Look!' But just then two powerful beams hit the beast square between the eyes.

'Wait!' I yelled over my shoulder, but it was too late. The remote control panel exploded in a puff of smoke and sparks and the Deinonychus toppled forward and crashed to the ground, its gaping jaw just centimetres from my face.

Darn it! Did Philly manage to see the map's coordinates? I wondered as the pigs joined me in the street and the roar of another monster sounded from beyond the buildings.

'Let's get out of here, before any more Remotosaurs turn up,' said Penelope, looking nervously around her.

'Wait a minute,' I said, remembering the thumping I'd heard coming from the Deinonychus across the street. I ran over to it, reaching for the penknife in my rucksack.

'Come on, Charlie,' cried Penelope. '*Weeh* haven't got time to muck about.'

'I won't be a mo,' I replied. The Deinonychus's stomach was still beating and I stuck the knife into the rubberized canvas skin and slit it open.

'*Oink!* Thanks, Charlie,' squealed Sage as he climbed out from inside the mechanized monster. 'I didn't think anyone could hear me thumping. I thought I was gonna be stuck in there forever!'

I grabbed the grateful porker's trotter and ran with him over to the others. They were delighted to see their friend again, but we had no time for reunions. We took to our heels and trotters, and ran through a series of side streets to the far edge of town where the pine trees stood near the base of the cliff.

I Fly Through The Air With The Greatest Of Ease!

As soon as we reached the trees, I took out the bag of wallow mud I'd stashed in my rucksack. Searching out all the small CCTV cameras I could find, I coated their lenses with the sticky gunk – I didn't want to be seen by any gamers at home and have them directing more Remotosaurs our way!

With my megashark's tooth, I sawed off a sturdy but springy branch from a nearby bush and cut a thin slit at each end with my penknife. I took a length of string from my explorer's kit and tied a large knot in each end of that. I jammed one end of the string into one of the slots and then, bending the branch over, slipped the other end of the string into the other slot to make a strong and powerful bow.

knot

string

springy branch

slit cut into branch

With that done, I fashioned an arrow from a stick. Using my knife and glue pen I carefully sliced up the giant owl feather I had in my rucksack and glued the pieces onto the stick to act as flights. At the other end I forced a piece of knapped flint into a slit and glued it in place for the arrowhead.

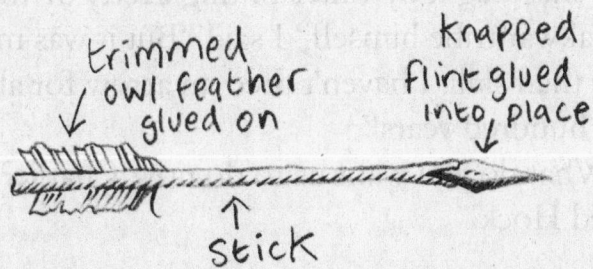

trimmed owl feather glued on

knapped flint glued into place

stick

The actual piece of flint I used →

With my bow and arrow complete, I tied a long, fine creeper to the arrow and prepared to fire. I aimed about three-quarters of the way up a thin, whippy tree, drew back the bow and, *thwack!* The arrow shot straight and true towards its mark and hit the tree with a shudder, embedding itself deep into the trunk.

'Great *grunt* shot!' gasped Sage in admiration.

'I was taught by Chief Sitting Pretty of the Rapakwar tribe himself,' I said. 'But it was more luck than skill. I haven't fired an arrow for about two hundred years!'

'What do you want us to do now, Charlie?' asked Hock.

'Grab this end of the creeper and pull for all you are worth,' I said and Hock ordered his troops to do as I'd asked.

They yanked and grunted, snorted and heaved. Gradually the tall, thin pine tree began to bend.

'Keep it up,' I encouraged, grabbing the creeper and lending a hand. Eventually the tree was bowed right over, its tip almost touching the ground. 'Hold it there!' I cried and ran over to the tree. I tied a heavier piece of creeper around the top and wound the other end around a stump in the ground and tied it tight.

'OK, you can let go now,' I said and the pigs stood back, puffing and burping from their exertion. The tree was now fixed to the ground in a great curve and all was ready for the next part of my plan.

'Very *oink* pretty, Charlie, but what is it for?' asked Penelope.

tree
creeper tied to stump

'Just watch,' I said. Facing the cliff face I climbed onto the end of the tree, gripping the trunk with my legs and hands. 'When I give the word, chop the creeper with your axe,' I said to Hock. 'Then stand back. If I make it, go and get the rest of your tribe and wait for me at the Maintenance Tunnel.'

'Will do,' said Hock. 'Good luck, Charlie.'

'Now!' I cried, closing my eyes and gritting my teeth in anticipation.

Hock raised his axe and *WHUMP!* He brought it slicing down onto the creeper. With a loud *twang* the creeper snapped, the tree whipped back up straight and tall, and I was catapulted high into the air, whizzing along at a hundred miles an hour.

'Gerronimo!' I cried as I whizzed out of control towards the cliff face. *Whack!* I hit it with a bone-crunching thump that knocked the wind out of me. My ray gun clattered to the ground below.

'Oof!' I whimpered. 'Perhaps that wasn't such a good idea.' But when I opened my eyes

Thunk!

I saw that I was clinging halfway up the cliff, well above the smooth, slippery lower section. Brilliant, my plan had worked! Giving my pals on the ground a thumbs-up, I began to climb upwards.

Gamer's Cliff Top Lair

A flock of Pterodactyls circled in the sky above and I prayed they wouldn't spot me. *I'm a sitting duck, stuck out on this exposed cliff face without my ray gun*, I thought, but I needn't have worried. The clever pigs below began firing at the soaring pests, and the terror birds swooped towards the warriors with grating squawks.

As a loud battle raged below me, I clambered steadily upwards. Twenty minutes later, I was perched just below one of the long windows of Nemesis Gamer's HQ.

I curled my fingers over the sill and slowly, quietly and carefully raised myself to peep inside, hoping that the ponytailed cretin wasn't looking out of the window at that precise moment. He wasn't – I don't know what I would've done if I'd found myself staring straight into his mean, pudgy face!

The windows were glazed with a thick pane of glass and on studying the frame I saw that they didn't open. Peering in, I saw a large room, the lower half of the back wall taken up with a bank of computer servers and, above those, hundreds of rows of tiny monitors. It looked as if the screens showed the faces of all the children around the world who were logged-on to play *Land of the Remotosaurs*. With brows puckered in concentration, they expertly manipulated their handheld controllers; some of them would be attacking my pig friends at this very moment.

Below the window was a long, curved desk filled with buttons, dials and more monitors. Lying on the desk was a half-eaten double cheeseburger that looked a couple of days old, so I reckoned that Nemesis hadn't been in the control room recently. *The whole system is probably set up to run on its own,* I thought. *Gamer would only have to check on things if there's a problem. I wonder where he is right now?*

I took the leather string that held the large diamond from around my neck. Using the diamond's sharp edge I scored a rectangular outline into the glass. (Diamonds are the hardest substance on earth and are often used as cutters and in drill bits – how handy that I have one!)

Then, with the heel of my palm, I gave the pane a hard thump and the rectangle of glass toppled onto the sill inside, leaving a gaping hole in the window.

Carefully I squeezed myself through the gap into the control room and jumped down to the floor. I was in! Now all I had to do was find Spriggot and get down to the Maintenance Tunnel to let the pigs in. Would they be ready in time, and would I bump into Nemesis Gamer?

An Amazing Discovery

The air was filled with a faint hum as computers whirred and lights flashed. The monitors on the wide desk displayed different areas of the stadium – parts of the ancient forest, the shore of Lake Woebetide and the Ghost Town. Some of the screens were black and I guessed these were from the cameras I had covered with mud.

I considered smashing the computers right away and putting an immediate stop to the dreadful game, but I was worried I might send the Remotosaurs into manic overdrive, setting them on an unstoppable path of destruction.

I decided to wait until all the pigs had been brought safely out of the stadium and into the tunnels.

On top of the control desk, next to the half-eaten hamburger, were some loose sheets of paper. They were photocopies of a magnificent diagram of the T-Rex Remotosaur, showing some of its workings and listing its full fighting capabilities. As there were so many of them, I thought it would be OK to take one, and I glued it straight in my journal. Over the page is the actual information sheet I found.

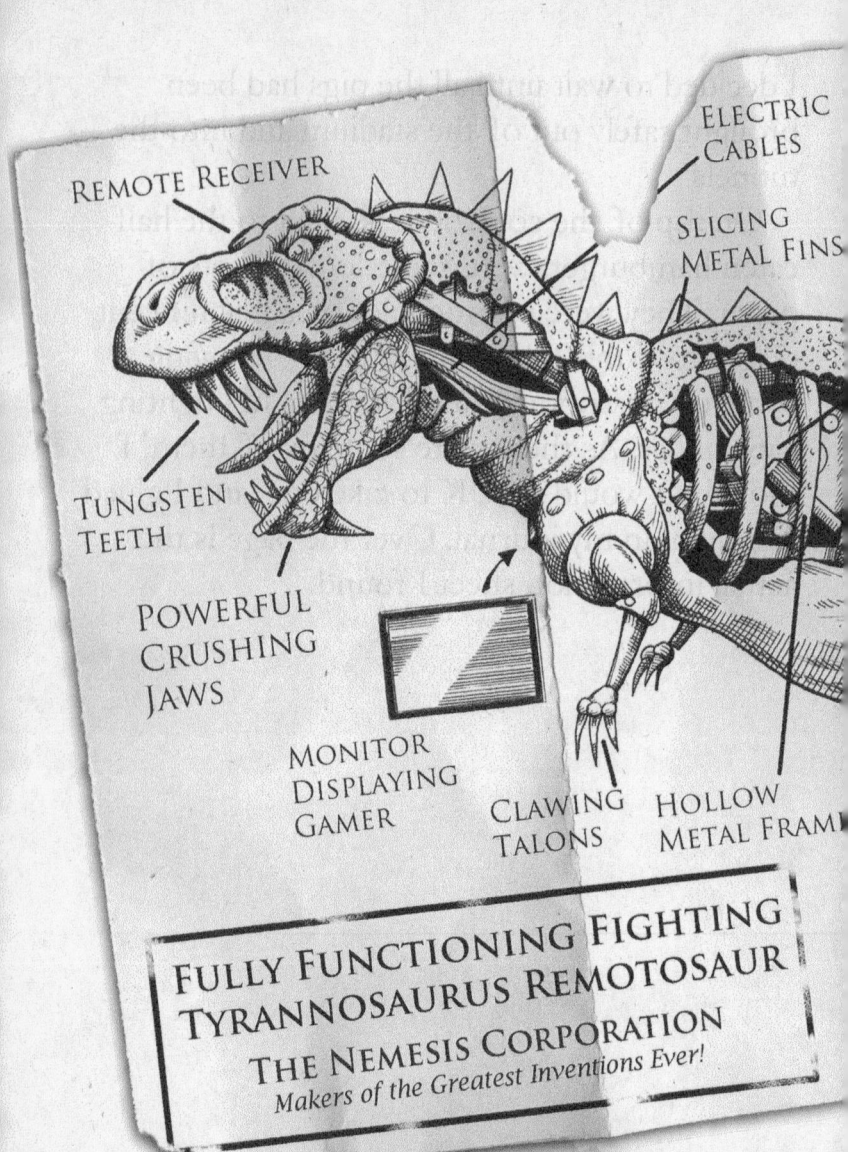

REMOTE RECEIVER

ELECTRIC CABLES

SLICING METAL FINS

TUNGSTEN TEETH

POWERFUL CRUSHING JAWS

MONITOR DISPLAYING GAMER

CLAWING TALONS

HOLLOW METAL FRAM

FULLY FUNCTIONING FIGHTING TYRANNOSAURUS REMOTOSAUR

THE NEMESIS CORPORATION

Makers of the Greatest Inventions Ever!

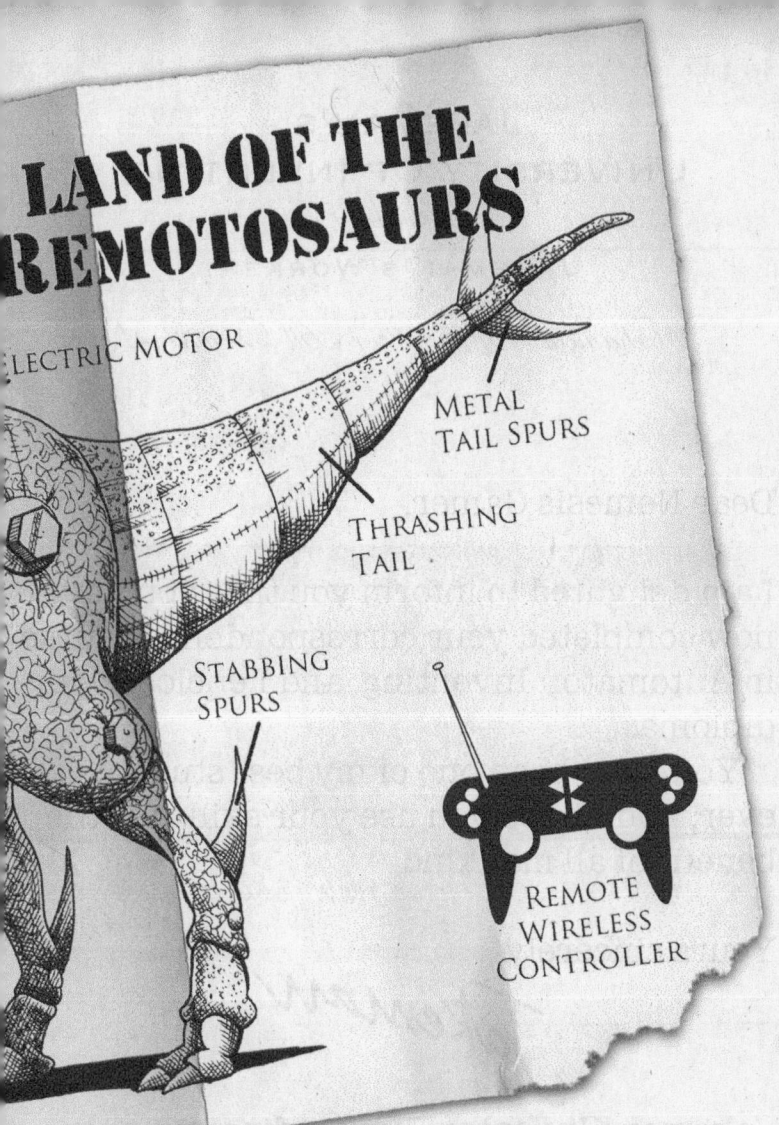

LAND OF THE REMOTOSAURS

ELECTRIC MOTOR

METAL
TAIL SPURS

THRASHING
TAIL

STABBING
SPURS

REMOTE
WIRELESS
CONTROLLER

Hidden amongst the photocopies was a typed letter, and I was just about to turn away uninterested, when I caught sight of the letterhead and snatched it up with a gasp.

JAKEMAN'S
UNIVERSITY OF INVENTING

A subsidiary of

JAKEMAN'S WORKS Ltd

Mechanical Marvels For All Occasions!

Dear Nemesis Gamer,

I am delighted to inform you that you have now completed your correspondence course in Automaton Inventing, and I enclose your diploma.

You have been one of my best students ever, and I hope you use your skills for the benefit of all mankind. *Yeah, right!*

Yours sincerely,

Jakeman

Jakeman (Inventor Extraordinaire)

I couldn't believe it! No wonder the Remotosaurs were so good – Nemesis Gamer had learned everything from my pal Jakeman. (He's the incredible inventor whose marvellous machines have saved me on so many of my adventures.) If Jakeman knew what Nemesis Gamer was doing with his expert knowledge, he would be devastated!

As I watched images of remote-controlled dinosaurs on the monitors, prowling the massive stadium in search of their poor piggy prey, I became even more determined to stop the evil games master.

Inside The Cliff

There was no sign of Spriggot in the room so I tiptoed over to the only door, turned the handle and inched it open. It led to a corridor and, after checking all was clear, I crept out, my ears straining for any sound of approaching danger.

The corridor opened out into a wide, circular space. In the centre, a winding staircase spiralled down to a lower floor. Beyond the stairs, sunlight streamed through a glass door in the curving outer wall and I rushed over, pushed it open and stepped out onto a metal balcony, high above the ground.

I was perched on the outside wall of the stadium and could see for miles and miles and miles – but there was no flight of stairs leading from the precarious platform to freedom – just a two hundred metre vertical drop. *Yikes!* I went back inside and tiptoed down the spiral staircase to the floor below, where I found myself in another corridor. A few chairs were placed along the sides, but otherwise it was as empty as the passageway upstairs.

I hurried along, eager to get my mission completed, my rubber-soled trainers hardly making a sound. I went pelting around a corner . . . and nearly crashed headlong into a lone, heavily-armoured Remotosaur! I'd never seen anything like it before, even in my books on dinosaurs. It was a low-slung, snub-nosed, armour-plated, grunting, growling brute that looked as if it would happily rip your leg off for a tasty, in-between meals treat. It was prowling the passageway like a grisly guard dog and with a squeak from my trainers, I leaped back around the corner.

I had another peep – the clanking creature was patrolling outside a door and I guessed it *might* be guarding poor old Spriggot. *The machine must be on automatic,* I thought. *Perhaps it reacts to movement.* As the dinosaur turned to face me, I ducked back behind the wall. The mechanical monster looked ferocious. What could I do? I looked around for inspiration.

On the ceiling above my head ran a row of utility pipes. I crept about ten metres back the way I'd come, placed one of the chairs in the middle of the corridor and climbed onto it. Then, taking a spare length of strong creeper from my rucksack, I threaded it over some of the pipes and let the two ends hang down either side. Quietly jumping to the floor, I tied a loop in one end of the creeper with a slipknot and opened it as wide as I could, with the bottom of the loop just touching the ground. The creeper was very springy, so the loop remained open in a big circle, about a metre and a half wide, like this:

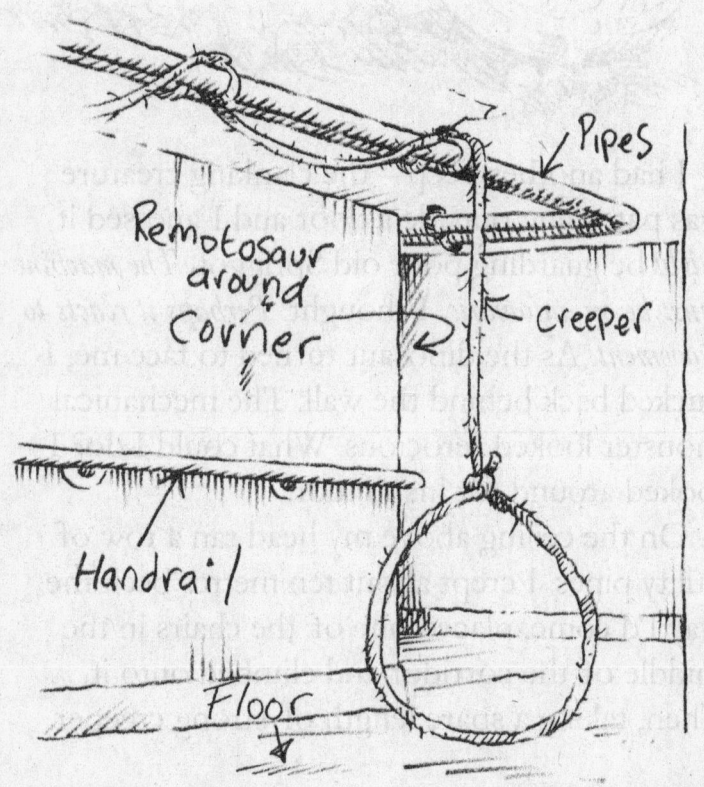

Remotosaur around Corner

Pipes

Creeper

Handrail

Floor

I grabbed the other end of the vine and threaded it through a bracket that held the pipes to the ceiling, a little further down the corridor. All was ready. *It should work,* I thought, *but my timing will have to be spot on.* With a gulp I crept back to the corner, stepped boldly out, waving my arms, and shouted, 'Hey, numbskull. Bet you can't catch me!'

The creature's eyes flashed when it registered my presence, and with a snarl and a whirr of motors, it lumbered towards me. I belted back the way I'd come, raced through the big loop of creeper and reached the dangling end of the vine just as the automatic guard skidded round the corner and came snapping after me.

As it dived through the loop I yanked hard on my end of the vine and the loop closed around the creature's bulky body. I heaved again, this time lifting the growling guard off the ground and right up to the ceiling, its four stubby legs flailing desperately in the air. I tied the end of the creeper to a handrail that ran the length of the corridor and then quickly ran under the dangling monster to the door it had been guarding.

The door wouldn't open, but I soon picked the lock with my skeleton key finger. I threw open the door and there, in the middle of the room, hanging in a sort of parrot cage suspended from the ceiling, was my friend Spriggot. He looked as grumpy as a grumpy old grouch who'd just come second in the world's grumpiest man competition!

'About time too. What kept yer?' the sprite said crossly, and I burst out laughing.

'I thought you might be pleased to see me,' I said.

'What d'yer want – a medal?' asked my bad-tempered buddy, his arms folded across his chest as he swung in his cage.

'Well, if you're going to be like that,' I said and pretended to leave.

'No, come back. I *am* pleased to see yer, OK? Please, open this bloomin' bird cage and get me out of here,' said Spriggot.

I had the cage unlocked

What kept yer?

Spriggot was locked in a bird cage!

in a second, Spriggot jumped down and we raced out of the room and continued along the corridor. I could hear the dangling guard snarling and scrabbling, and hoped the creeper wouldn't snap. We turned another corner and the passage came to a halt at the doors to a lift.

~~A Secret~~ Nemesis Again

I pressed the button to call the lift and the motor clanged into operation.

'What's the plan, Charlie?' asked Spriggot in his buzzy voice as we waited.

'We're going to find the doors to the Maintenance Tunnel and let in the Pig Troopers,' I explained. 'Hock should've rounded them all up by now and they should be waiting outside.' The lift arrived and we got in.

As we descended, I explained everything that had happened since Gamer had whisked the little sprite away.

'Wow!' said an amazed Spriggot. 'And once we've let the pigs in, what then?'

'We destroy Gamer's computers and stop

this game forever,' I said. 'Then we can look for a way out of here.'

'If you say so,' said Spriggot, looking cross again.

'What's wrong now?' I asked.

'Can't we just find a way out and escape?' grumbled the little fellow. 'Is it worth riskin' our lives for a bunch of silly old pigs?'

'Spriggot!' I cried. 'How could you think such a thing? The pigs are brave and true friends. We can't just leave them to Gamer and the Remotosaurs!'

'Keep yer hair on,' said Spriggot. 'It was just an idea. If they're friends of yours, I suppose we should save 'em.'

Just then the lift shook as we reached the ground floor and the doors slowly opened. A dim tunnel disappeared to the left and right.

TO THE STADIUM

TO THE STOREROOM & EXIT

'Brilliant!' I whispered softly to my friend. 'This way, Spriggot.' I stepped out of the lift towards the stadium . . . and stopped in my tracks. Help – blocking our path was Nemesis Gamer! I don't know who was more surprised!

'You!' he wheezed, reaching for his ray gun.

In the blink of an eye, Spriggot sprang from the ground and karate-kicked the gun from Gamer's hand. It went spinning down the corridor behind him, but Nemesis Gamer was surprisingly quick himself and his hand snatched Spriggot from the air and held him tight.

'Let him go, you creep!' I yelled, launching myself into a flying rugby-tackle and bringing the man crashing to the ground.

'Ooof!' he yelled letting go of Spriggot as

he fell, but he recovered quickly and before I had time to disentangle myself from his legs, he grabbed my hand, pulled a set of handcuffs from his long coat and clamped them around my wrist. 'Got you, you interfering little maggot,' he hissed in his whispering, snake-like voice.

'Go, Spriggot,' I yelled, hoping he would dash for the maintenance doors and let the pigs in.

'Yes, run little man, run, or I'll squash you like a bug!' sneered Gamer.

In a series of lightning dashes, the little chap disappeared along the corridor – towards the exit!

'Oh no!' I groaned in disbelief.

'Good riddance, grumpy little devil,' hissed Nemesis Gamer. 'I won't miss him – what a moaner!' He got up and dragged me to my feet. 'It's back inside the stadium for you, my friend. You've proved quite an attraction with the gamers so far and, sooner or later, one of them will get you. *Sss-sss-sss!*'

Nemesis Gamer manhandled me along the tunnel in the direction of the stadium. This was brilliant! He was taking me to the tunnel doors himself.

'I don't know how you got in here, Charlie,' Gamer whispered. 'But you don't stand a chance against the great Nemesis Gamer.'

'You're not that great,' I said. 'You've learned everything from my pal Jakeman, the great inventor.'

'So, Jakeman's a pal of yours, is he?' spat Gamer in a hoarse whisper. 'Well, he's a pea-brain compared to me, *sss-sss*. I am the greatest inventor ever, and this stadium is just the start. There's another being constructed right now, where robotic Megasaurs, driven by real live humans, will engage in battle. It'll make the Roman gladiatorial games of old seem like a stroll in the park. *Sss-sss-ssssss!*'

The nutty nitwit continued his ravings. 'No one's ever appreciated my genius, but soon they'll have to,' he said, a froth of spittle forming on his lips. 'Anyone who's ever annoyed me will be thrown into the stadium to take their chances. People will come from all over the world to watch and my new games will make me the richest, most powerful man in the world. *Ha ha ha ha ha ha!*'

'You're a nutter,' I said as we reached the big arched doors that led into the stadium.

'Yeah, whatever. You're the one that's going to end up as mechanical dinosaur's grub,' sniggered Nemesis, undoing my handcuffs. He pulled a lever that drew back the bolts on the door and opened it, just wide enough to push me through. 'So long, Charlie Small, nice knowing you – *not!*'

'CHARGE, *grunt!*' came a guttural cry from outside and the doors were smashed wide open by a hundred stampeding pigs.

'What the . . .!' cried Nemesis Gamer as a line of furious pigs charged in, and with remarkable speed for such a small, tubby man, he turned on his heels and scarpered before anyone had chance to grab him. As he disappeared along the tunnel, he called out, '*Hee hee!* Watch out for my surprises, little piggies!'

What a nutter!

Surprise, Surprise!

'Everyone in,' I cried, holding the door as all the squeaking and squealing pigs piled through. We heard a roar from a Remotosaur, and as the last pig made it inside, I slammed the door and lifted the lever to throw the bolts. I was only just in time for, as the bolts slid into place, the doors shook with a mighty crash as the attacking Remotosaur threw all its weight at them.

'Phewee!' squealed Penelope. 'That was close. That one has been stalking us for the last hour.'

'It's good to see you,' I said to all the pigs. 'Let's go and smash the computers before Nemesis Gamer has time to make his next move.'

'What did he mean, watch out for my surprises *oink* – what surprises?' asked Hock, brandishing his ray gun and looking along the dark tunnel after Gamer.

'I've no idea,' I said. ' Just keep your eyes peeled and your ears . . . *Whoa,* Watch out!'

A trickle of falling rust landed on my shoe and made me look up at the ceiling, just in time to see something move in the shadows.

'Dive!' I yelled, pushing the pigs in front of me. We rolled across the ground as a heavy iron boulder dropped from a chute above. It landed with an earth-shaking thud, just where we'd been standing!

'There's one of his surprises for you,' I cried. 'Come on!'

CRASH!

Hock and I led the crowd of pigs, with Penelope and Sage taking up the rear. Some of the baby pigs started sniffling and crying. 'Don't worry,' I said. 'We'll be all right.'

'Duck!' snorted Hock all of a sudden, and we dropped to the ground just as a roaring flame shot across the tunnel from a nozzle in the wall, singeing the feather on Hock's helmet. The flame roared for a few seconds and then died and we breathed a collective sigh of relief.

'Bloomin' heck, we were nearly crackling then!' gasped the pig's leader.

We carried on more cautiously than ever, scanning the ceiling, walls and floor as we went. Then, 'Stop!' I cried as two shiny blades swept from narrow slits on either side of the tunnel like a pair of giant's scissors. They sliced through the air with a horrible swishing sound before disappearing back into their slots. As I edged a toe forward, the blades swiped again, nearly taking the tip from my trainer.

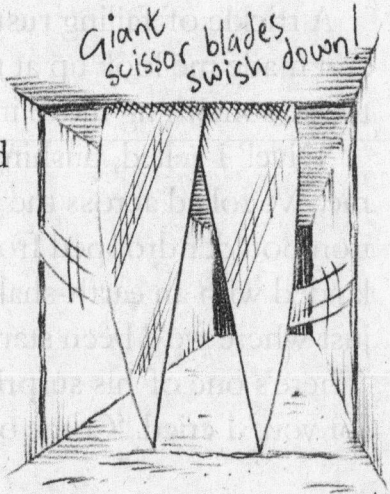

Giant scissor blades swish down!

'We can't go on,' I said. 'Every time I edge forward, it sets off the blades.'

'Could we dart through, one by one?' asked Hock.

'We could try, but I don't think we'd all make it,' I said, studying the deadly device. 'Somehow we've got to try and jam those blades.' I had a flash of inspiration.

'Just a minute, this might work,' I said, taking my super-strength glue pen from my explorer's kit. I carefully sliced off the ball tip with my penknife.

'Stand back, everyone,' I said and tentatively edged the toe of my trainer forward.

Swish! The scissors sliced down from either side and I squeezed the tube as hard as I could, squirting the gunky contents across the blades. As the curved cutters overlapped, the glue was smeared between them and the blades stuck fast.

'It worked!' I said. Then a grinding, groaning sound of machinery started up and the blades began to vibrate and shudder. 'Quickly everyone, get past before the glue gives way,' I cried.

We sent the piglets past the straining blades

in quick succession. Then Hock, myself and the rest of the troopers dashed through. Penelope brought up the rear and, as she pushed her way past the jammed scissors, *thwack!* the blades flew open as the glue was ripped asunder. One of the swinging blades caught Penelope's trailing trotter and she was thrown into the air, landing with an echoing thump on the steel floor.

'My goodness,' she puffed. 'That's one heck of a bacon slicer!'

The pigs laughed with relief. We had all made it safely past the scything scissors and we reached the lift without any more of Nemesis's surprises.

'I think we might be over the worst,' I said, pressing the button to open the doors.

Megasaur

But just then a terrible noise erupted from further along the tunnel. A strong beam of light cut through the gloom and we saw the most terrifying sight of all. From the direction of the storeroom and completely filling the tunnel, appeared a massive, metallic, skeletal dinosaur.

Perched on a seat in the back of the monster,
pulling levers and grinning like a madman, was
Nemesis Gamer himself.

'Meet Megasaur,
the prototype
of my next
range of
Remotosaur,
Charlie,' cried
Nemesis above
the clunking,
banging and
whirring
machinery. 'Soon
millions of kids will
be driving one
of these in
real gladiatorial battles. Neat, eh? *Sss-sss-sss.*'
He pulled a lever and the metal joints in the
creature's neck flexed and curved, shooting
its mighty jaw forward and snapping a row of
crushing molars. 'Quite a handful, I think you'll
agree. Ha ha ha!'

Hock dropped to one knee and drew his ray
gun. The rest of the troopers dropped to the
ground, guns at the ready. 'Fire!' yelled Hock.

Mad Nemesis

Zap, zap, zap! Fifty red beams struck the Megasaur and, fizzing and sparking, bounced harmlessly off its massive, riveted body.

'You'll have to do better than that, my little suckling pigs,' sneered Gamer as he continued to get closer. 'Watch this!'

He pressed a button and *boof, boof!* two crackling, electric balls shot from the Megasaur's empty eye-sockets, exploding into flame as they hit the ground in front of us.

'Jeepers!' I cried. 'We don't stand a chance.'

'Here, Charlie. Go for its eyes,' yelled Hock, tossing me a spare ray gun as another pair of sparking spheres exploded into flame, making the air around us as hot as an oven. 'Quick, before we're all cooked!'

Zap, zap, zap! We fired and fired, our beams hitting the machine's eyeless sockets. Another two spheres shot out, but they veered off at tangents, ricocheting like deadly balls from the walls and floor.

'It's working!' grunted Sage and we continued to strafe the target. *Zap, zap!*

'You porcine pests,' hissed Gamer, pressing the firing button over and over to no effect. 'You've broken it. Never mind, it'll have to be minced pork for tea instead of grilled chops!' And thrusting the drive levers forward, he sent the Megasaur lumbering towards us.

The machine's metal feet sent echoing crashes along the tunnel. Its great, hinged legs hissed with hydraulics and its articulated neck swept its grinning skull from one side of the tunnel to the other.

Suddenly the head darted forward and, with a snap of it chops, caught Hock by the arm and lifted him from the floor, ready to flip him inside its crushing jaws.

'Help!' squealed Hock.

I fired my ray gun, hitting the monster's mechanical head side on and blasting it against the tunnel wall with a crash. The levers jumped from Gamer's hands and Hock dropped from the Megasaur's mouth.

'Right, I've had enough of you, you interfering insect, Charlie Small,' spat Gamer, grabbing the levers again and turning the monster's head towards me. It loomed over me; the great mouth opened; the teeth glistened. I closed my eyes and waited for the crushing pressure of the Megasaur's munching mandibles.

Boof! Boof! Boof! A shower of crackling fire-pellets hit the Megasaur from behind, whipping its legs from under it and sending it crashing to the ground. When Nemesis pulled desperately on a lever to try to make the massive mechanoid stand, a leg detached at the hip and the Megasaur rolled over, sending Gamer spinning across the floor.

'What's going on?' screamed the shaken games master.

Staring back down the tunnel we saw an extraordinary sight – a fat mosquito, about a metre long, was flying towards us and shooting a stream of flaming pellets from its long, tapering proboscis. Sitting in the open cockpit in the creature's back was Spriggot, frantically pulling at levers with a determined look on his wrinkled face!

'Go, Spriggot, go!' I yelled. The manic metal mosquito bumped crazily from one side of the tunnel to the other as it continued to spray the collapsed Megasaur with pellets. 'Whoa! Careful, Spriggot,' I cried as a flurry of shots whizzed past my ear. Behind me, Gamer picked himself up and dived into the waiting lift.

'See you, suckers!' he cried as the lift doors swished closed and he disappeared.

'Help! I can't control this stupid thing,' shouted Spriggot as the mozzie buzzed past us and carried on towards Nemesis Gamer's booby traps.

'Quick, Spriggot. Jump!' I yelled. The sprite stood up in his seat and launched himself from the back of the Mosquito, landing on top of me and knocking me to the ground. Seconds later, *swish!* The booby trap blades of the slicing scissors sprang into action and carved the mozzie clean in half! The tunnel became silent apart from our breathing and a few whimpers from some of the piglets.

'Well done, Spriggot,' I said, but the little chap didn't answer. He had fainted with shock!

Spriggot The Hero!

I knelt down and patted his face and the sprite slowly came round.

'Feeling better?' I asked as he sat up and I gave him a drink from the water bottle in my rucksack.

'Oh, marvellous,' moaned the sprite in his usual grouch. 'Couldn't be better. I mean who wouldn't be all right after nearly getting mangled in a mechanical mosquito.'

'Where did you find it?' I asked.

'It was in Gamer's storeroom. I was hiding there when he rushed in and drove away one of those Megasaur things,' said the sprite. 'I knew he was up to no good and I thought I'd better try and stop him.'

'Well, you were very brave,' I said. 'Thanks for coming back for us.'

'Yes *grunt* thanks indeed, Spriggot, *oink*. You're as brave as any Pig Trooper,' grunted Hock and all the others squealed in agreement. Spriggot beamed with pride.

'I really think we ought to be going now, Charlie,' continued the pigs' leader. 'Before Nemesis Gamer comes back with an even more dangerous adversary.'

'You're right,' I said. 'We're not out of danger yet.' Then, pressing the lift button again, I added, 'Hock, you must lead your pigs out of the tunnel to freedom. I'm going back to the control room to smash the computers.'

'I'll come,' said Spriggot.

'And take Spriggot with you,' I said. 'He's done enough today.'

'You can't go alone,' said Hock. 'Let *weeh* me help.'

'I'll come,' buzzed Spriggot.

'No,' I said to the pigs' leader. 'Your troopers need you. Anyway, this mission will be best tackled alone.'

'Is no one listenin' to me? I said, *I'll come,*' yelled Spriggot.

'I'm sorry, Spriggot, but you must go with the pigs,' I said. 'You're not strong enough. You just fainted, for goodness sakes.'

'All right, if you don't want me to, I won't,' said the grumpy man, folding his arms and turning his back on me.

'Oh, Spriggot,' I said, frustrated. Just then the lift arrived and the doors opened.

'Come on *grunt,* Spriggot, Charlie knows what he's doing,' said Hock, taking the sprite's hand. 'We'll see you on the outside, Charlie. Good luck.' Then he led Spriggot down the tunnel at a trot, followed by the rest of the pigs.

'Take care, Charlie,' cried Penelope as they disappeared towards the exit.

'*Weeh, weeh, weeh,*' squealed the piglets. Soon they were out of sight, and I stepped into the lift and pressed the button that would take me up to the control room, where I knew Nemesis Gamer was likely to be waiting for me.

Hanging On For Dear Life!

The lift rattled and hummed as it climbed upwards. I began to feel uneasy. *Something's not quite right*, I thought. All of a sudden the lift shuddered to a halt and, *BANG!* The floor beneath me suddenly dropped open and I fell through it like a stone. I made a desperate grab for the handrail that ran around the inside of the lift.

'Got it!' I cried, as my fingertips curled around the bar. I found myself swinging above the deep shaft that disappeared into gloomy depths. I managed to find a narrow foothold running around the base of the lift and hauled myself onto it. Now I could reach the UP button and I pressed it again, but the lift didn't move. *Flip*, I thought.

What can I do now? I looked up and saw there was a light-fitting protruding from the wall above my head. Teetering on the narrow foothold, I stretched for it, but it was too high.

Calling on every shred of courage I possessed, I bent my knees and leaped for the light-fitting. If I missed, I would plummet down the lift shaft and end up as strawberry jam – but my hands just managed to clamp themselves around the bracket and I hung there for a moment, swinging back and forth like a human pendulum.

The rucksack on my back felt heavy and I started to sweat from effort and fear as I swung my feet up onto the handrail, then pulled myself upright so the lift's ceiling was just above me. I pushed against one of the ceiling panels and flipped it to one side. Now I could see two thick cables attached to the heavy frame of the lift. They rose up the shaft and I knew they were my only means of escape.

I clambered through the roof onto the top of the lift and, taking a deep breath, began to climb the cables. My shoulder hurt, but I was an expert climber. (After all, I was crowned king of the gorillas!) Hand over hand I shinned up the steel cables, my palms becoming sore and blistered.

I soon reached the doors on the top level. They were firmly shut, but by blasting a fuse box inside the shaft with a bolt from my ray gun, the doors clanked open. I swung myself across the gap and landed in the empty corridor. The guard dinosaur was no longer dangling from the ceiling and was nowhere to be seen.

I ran full pelt down the passage to the spiral stairs and mounted them two at a time. Seconds later I was back at the control room, and I gently opened the door and peered inside. The computers were still beeping and humming; the monitors on the wide, curved desk flashed with images of Remotosaurs vainly looking for prey, but otherwise the room was quiet and empty.

I stepped inside and drew my ray gun, ready to blast the bank of machinery and put an end to the deadly *Land of the Remotosaurs* game.

Show Down

'*Sss-sss-sss, I'll* take that, thank you,' hissed Gamer from behind the door.

Darn it! I thought. I slowly turned around. Nemesis Gamer grinned, flourishing an evil-looking machine ray gun. 'Drop your gun and kick it over to me,' he sneered.

'Run, Charlie!' buzzed a familiar voice as, in a blur of colour, Spriggot flashed into the room and dived at Gamer.

'No, Spriggot, he's armed,' I yelled.

Taken unawares, Gamer span around, firing his automatic. Spriggot hit him like a little ball of fury, wrapping himself around Gamer's arm as the machine gun spluttered and spat, *zazazazazap!* The beams swept across the room, strafing the control desk until it collapsed in a puff of smoke. Gamer shook Spriggot off and the tiny sprite went flying behind the bank of mainframe computers at the back of the room, landing with a crash and a bad-tempered curse.

I dived after him and we crouched in the narrow gap between the machines and the back wall, waiting for Gamer's next move. There was silence from the room. What was he up to?

'Thanks, Spriggot. Where did you spring from?' I whispered as we crept further behind the machines for cover.

'I thought you might need my help so I left the pigs and climbed after you,' said the sprite with a grin. Above our heads the multitude of monitors flickered as gamers played *Land of the Remotosaurs*. Well, I was playing it for real – and I seemed to be in a losing situation.

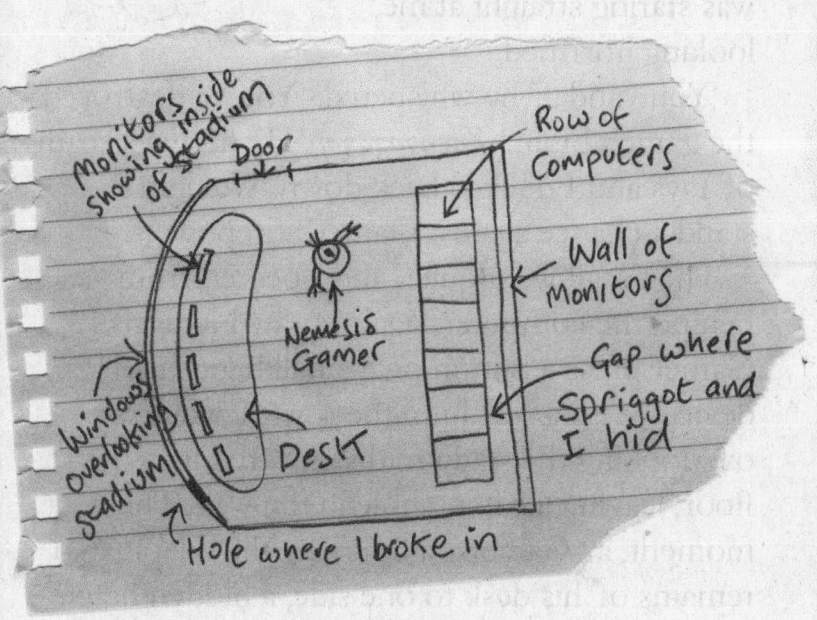

'Come out, Charlie. You can't escape, you know,' hissed Gamer's voice.

'Maybe not, but I can put a stop to your evil games,' I said and fired my ray gun at the back of the computers. One by one they popped and crackled until the room was full of billowing smoke. All the monitors went blank.

'How do you like that?' I cried, raising my head above the smoking machines. *Whoops!* Gamer was staring straight at me, looking horrified.

'You vandal,' he whispered. 'You've destroyed the game's brain.' *Zazazazazap!* He fired a stream of rays and I ducked back down. We didn't stand a chance against Gamer's firepower.

Then it all went quiet, and I peered from behind the computers again. I saw Nemesis Gamer press a button on a small hand-held device. With a soft hum the row of windows overlooking the stadium disappeared into the floor, leaving a gaping hole in the wall. The next moment, as Gamer was shoving the dilapidated remains of his desk to one side, a hidden hatch opened in the ceiling and a strange, tubular metal contraption was lowered to the floor.

'What the heck is that?' whispered Spriggot.

Still covering us with his machine gun, Gamer sat down in the contraption's small seat and pulled a lever. Two huge black wings spread out above his head.

'It's a microlight – a sort of motorized hang-glider,' I gasped.

Nemesis pressed another button and an ominous, loud ticking noise began. 'So long, Charlie Small,' he sneered. 'My *Land of the Remotosaurs* game is over and it's time for me to go, *sss-sss-sss* – but not you my friend. You must stay and see it through to the end. I've set a self-destruct device in operation that will go off in – oooh, fifteen minutes. Can you hear it tick, tick, tick? *Hee hee hee.* All my wonderful inventions, *boom!* They will go up like a rocket. It doesn't matter – I will be able to start again. But you, dear boy, will be atomized. *Hee hee hee hee!*'

'You're completely bonkers,' I said.

'Whatever,' hissed Gamer as he started the microlight's motor and a small propeller behind his seat whirred into life. 'So long, Charlie

Small.' The craft lurched forward, out through the gaping hole in the wall and dropped from sight. The next moment it was climbing with a whine towards the glass roof.

'Come back, you can't leave us to be blown to smithereens!' I yelled, running to the edge of the opening. But with a staccato of zaps from his machine gun, Nemesis Gamer blew a hole through the roof and flew out of the stadium and away. Suddenly his pre-recorded voice crackled through some hidden speakers. 'Eight minutes and counting', it said matter-of-factly. 'I lied about the fifteen minutes!' *Tick, tick, tick!*

Eight minutes and counting...

Get Me Out Of Here!

'What a creep! We've only got eight minutes before the bomb goes off,' I said. 'Let's go!' We raced down the corridor but as we reached the top of the spiral stairs a loud bellow rumbled up from the floor below. I crept halfway down, only to see the guard robot that I'd last seen dangling from my loop of vine, snarling at the foot of the stairs. It didn't seem to be able to climb them, but our escape route was well and truly blocked.

'Six minutes and counting!' the speaker informed us. *Tick, tick, tick.*

'Oh, shut up, I'm trying to think,' I yelled. There was nothing for it; we would have to take the only way remaining to us.

'Come on, Spriggot, we're going to have to climb down the cliff face,' I said, pointing to where the glass door led out onto the balcony.

'We'll never make it in time,' the little man cried.

'That's a chance we'll have to take,' I said.

Just then a loud roar sounded from *outside* as the glass door slammed open in a strong blast of wind. *What now?* I wondered. Surely there couldn't be another monster attacking from out there? I scampered nervously over to have a look, but couldn't see anything unusual. I stepped out onto the metal balcony and peered through my telescope.

In the distance I could see Hock and some of his Pig Troopers marching back towards the stadium. He had realized something was up and was coming back with a rescue squad.

Some of the Pig Troopers were marching back

'Stay away,' I yelled at him. 'This whole place is going to blow!' but they were much too far away to hear me.

'Four minutes and counting!'

Whoa! That woke me up.

'Time to go, Spriggot,' I said swinging a leg over the balustrade.

ROAR!

Whoa, there it was again – and this time the

noise was so loud I jumped in shock, nearly losing my footing and tumbling over the side.

Explosion

'What's that?' gasped Spriggot, shaking with fear.

'Oh my goodness,' I cried, for ten metres above us was a large, striped balloon with a cigar-shaped silver pod hanging underneath. It was my pal Jakeman's Space Balloon! Good old Philly must have read the map coordinates and they'd come to rescue me.

The Space Balloon hovered above me

'Help!' I cried as the blast from the propeller subsided and the balloon hovered silently above us. 'I'm here, just below you! And there's a bomb about to go off!' But they obviously couldn't hear me, for a loudhailer crackled into life and I heard Jakeman's voice booming:

'Testing, testing; is this thing on, Theo? Oh! . . . Right, here goes. WE'VE WORKED OUT WHAT YOU'RE UP TO, NEMESIS GAMER! If I'd known what you were like I would *never* have taught you inventing. You must be as mad as a box of monkeys. Now, stop this gaming nonsense, GIVE YOURSELF UP!'

'Two minutes and counting!' the time-bomb voice informed us.

'Jakeman, it's me, Charlie Small,' I yelled.

'Oh Charlie, we're done for,' whimpered Spriggot. 'I knew I should've stayed in my tree!'

'IF YOU'RE NOT OUT IN FIVE MINUTES, WE'RE COMING TO GET YOU!' continued Jakeman.

Oh no you're not, I thought. *In five minutes time you'll have been blasted into the middle of next week!* I slipped off my rucksack and fumbled around inside. I'd just remembered, the Space Balloon had an onboard telephone – and I knew the number!

I grabbed my mobile and punched in the numbers, praying it still had enough charge.

'I'M WAITING,' continued Jakeman. 'I KNOW YOU . . . Oh bother, who's that ringing now?' With a crackle, the loudhailer went off.

'Whoever it is, I'm busy,' said Jakeman in his normal voice, answering the phone.

'It's me, Charlie Small,' I yelled.

'Charlie, you're safe! Philly was worried that her Remotosaur had squashed you flat!' cried Jakeman, sounding delighted.

'One minute and counting!'

'Who said that?' asked Jakeman. 'Where are you, Charlie?'

'I'm right below you. Hurry up and get out of here! This whole place is going to blow up!' I stammered.

'Right below us? But we're . . . hold on, Charlie. Stay where you are!'

A few seconds later, the doors to the silver capsule slid open and Philly was standing there, hair blowing in the wind.

'Come on, Charlie!' she yelled and threw a rope ladder over the side.

'After you,' I said to Spriggot and we both raced up into the capsule as fast as we could.

'Thirty seconds and counting,' said the voice from the stadium as the doors slid shut.

'Quick, get as far away as you can!' I cried as Philly gave me a welcoming hug.

Philly's mum, Harmonia, was in the pilot's seat and she threw a switch to open a valve that sent extra gas pumping into the balloon above. We started to rise, quicker and quicker as I counted off the seconds in my head. *Five, four, three, two, one . . .* I waited . . .

BOOM!

We heard a massive explosion and all of us, Jakeman and Spriggot, Philly and Theo, Harmonia and myself, sat holding our breaths. For a second nothing happened, then *whoosh!*

our capsule was rocketed through the air on the shockwave from the enormous blast. It span and rocked, flipped and turned and we were sent sprawling across the small cabin, landing in a tangled pile.

There was a loud, rushing sound of wind as if we were at the heart of a tornado, and the raging sky outside the spinning window made the interior of our capsule glow bright orange.

'Ouch! Yeeow! Oof!' everyone yelled as we tumbled about like clothes in a drier. 'Get your foot out of my ear,' I heard someone say.

'If you get your elbow out of my eye,' someone else replied.

Then, as quickly as it began, our rocketing, rumbustious ride stopped and we hung serenely, high in the sky, from our stripy balloon once more.

Catching Our Breath

'Phew!' said Jakeman. 'Is everyone OK?'

'A few bruises, Grandpa, nothing more,' said Philly rubbing her elbow.

'We're fine,' said Harmonia and Theo.

'Oh dear,' cried Jakeman rushing over to the small window. 'What about Nemesis Gamer? I know he was a wrong 'un, but he didn't deserve to be blasted into eternity like that.'

We peered down to where the stadium had once stood and saw a frazzled area of smoking ruins and blackened tree stumps.

'Don't worry about Nemesis Gamer,' I said. 'He's miles away by now. It was him who set the thing off.'

'My forest,' gasped Spriggot. 'He's obliterated my ancient homeland.'

'Why would he blow his own games stadium up?' asked Theo.

'Well, Spriggot and I sort of destroyed his control centre,' I said.

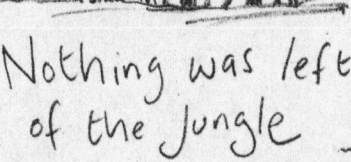

Nothing was left of the jungle

'The poor pigs he used as targets had escaped and his computers were smoking like chimneys, so he decided to cut and run.'

'Those pigs were real?' gasped Philly. 'What a fiend! I never realized that when I was playing the game. Grandpa only bought it for my birthday because he'd taught the game's inventor. I thought it was all computer graphics. Imagine my surprise when I saw you waving that map at me!'

'Imagine my surprise when I saw you on a screen, sending a dinosaur to eat me!' I said. 'It wasn't funny!'

'I just had enough time to see the map's coordinates before my Remotosaur got zapped and my game was over,' said Philly.

'When Philly told me you were inside the game, I put two and two together and didn't like the answer; so we set out to rescue you,' said Jakeman. 'Well done, Charlie. You've stopped an evil genius in his tracks. And well done to your new friend too!' He patted a very proud Spriggot on the shoulder and shook my hand warmly. 'Now, let's get you two back to the factory for a meal and a good night's sleep.'

'It's good to have you back, Charlie,' said Philly with a grin.

'We're so glad you survived your fall from the prop shaft,' said Harmonia.

'Yes, sorry about that, Charlie,' said Theo, looking slightly embarrassed.

'It's brilliant to be back,' I said. 'You do want to come with us, don't you, Spriggot?'

The little chap was still staring wistfully down at his ruined forest. 'Huh,' he said, folding his arms and scowling. 'I haven't got anywhere else to go, have I?'

'Great,' said Jakeman with a smile. 'All hands on deck. Increase pressure, Theo. Full speed ahead, Harmonia.'

'Oh, before we go, can we check on the pigs?' I asked.

'But of course. How remiss of me,' gasped Jakeman. 'We must make sure they're OK first.'

Destination Jakeman's Factory

Harmonia steered the Space Balloon down to the plain below the stadium. The ground was littered with chunks of metal and bits of

Remotosaur, and there hiding behind a ridge of high ground and staring in disbelief at the devastation were Hock and his brave Pig Troopers.

I opened the capsule doors as Harmonia lowered the balloon to hover about ten metres from the ground.

'Don't worry, Hock. It's Charlie!' I yelled as the pigs cowered below us, staring up at the strange silver pod and stripy balloon. It must've seemed like some strange alien being come to attack their hiding place.

'Charlie? Oh *grunt* good you made it out in time my brave *weeh* friend. I was coming to *oink* find you when the building blew,' grunted Hock. 'Is Spriggot OK?'

'Spriggot's fine. Where are you going to go now?' I replied, my voice being snatched away on the buffeting wind.

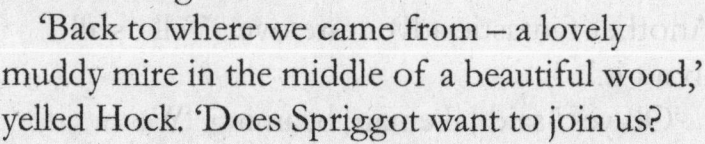

Hock gazed up at us!

'Back to where we came from – a lovely muddy mire in the middle of a beautiful wood,' yelled Hock. 'Does Spriggot want to join us?

There are some huge oaks there.'

'Well?' I asked the sprite. 'Would you rather go with the pigs?' I could see by his bright, shining eyes that he would.

'Oh Charlie,' he said, his voice buzzing with excitement. 'It sounds great. Would you mind?'

'Of course not, silly,' I said. 'It sounds just the place for you.'

So the little forest sprite thanked Jakeman and all his family for rescuing him and then leaped up and threw his arms around my neck.

'Thanks for everything,' he buzzed, and before I could reply he jumped down, leaped out of the capsule and did a back somersault to land safely on the ground amongst his new piggy pals.

'Goodbye!' I called out as the balloon lifted us higher into the sky and the propeller whizzed into life.

'Goodbye,' the pigs and Spriggot called as we cruised away, our tiny shadow following us along the ground far below.

'So, Charlie,' said Philly when the doors had been closed and we'd left the stadium far behind. 'Another fantastic adventure over. Tell us all about it.'

'Oh yes,' said Jakeman, beaming. 'Wait a bit,

though.' He turned a calibrated dial and pulled down a heavy lever. 'Course set for Nor' by Nor' West; cruising speed, ten knots. Put the kettle on, Theo – we'll have a nice cuppa while Charlie tells his story. Next stop, Jakeman's Factory!'

Yippee!

It's an hour or so later. I've told my pals all my adventures inside the gaming stadium and I'm busy bringing my journal up to date before we get back to the factory. As soon as we arrive, Jakeman will be able to send me home. I can't wait! Surely nothing can go wrong now . . .

CRASH!

Whoa! Hold on, something's happening. *Our space pod's been hit.*

BOOF!

Yikes! We've been hit again. Everybody's yelling. Smoke is pouring from the controls. Hold on, I'm going to try and get to the window.

Oh, no! A black winged microlight is buzzing towards us. It's got rocket launchers on each wing and strapped in the pilot's seat is a grinning Nemesis Gamer, his finger hovering over a launch button. NO!

WHOOSH!

KERBOOM!

Boof!

PUBLISHER'S NOTE

This is where Charlie's tenth journal ends.
Will he and his friends survive Gamer's aerial
attack and make it back to Jakeman's Factory?
Will he ever get home to his mum and dad in
time for tea? Is there another fantastic journal
just waiting to be found? Keep your eyes
peeled and your trigger fingers ready!

www.charliesmall.co.uk

manic RemotoSaur! ©Charlie Small

My idea for a mad,

Sensors to detect movement and body heat

Remote Control recei

Steel horns

steel m skin

Tungsten, tearing teeth

Crushir Jaws

can fire laser beams

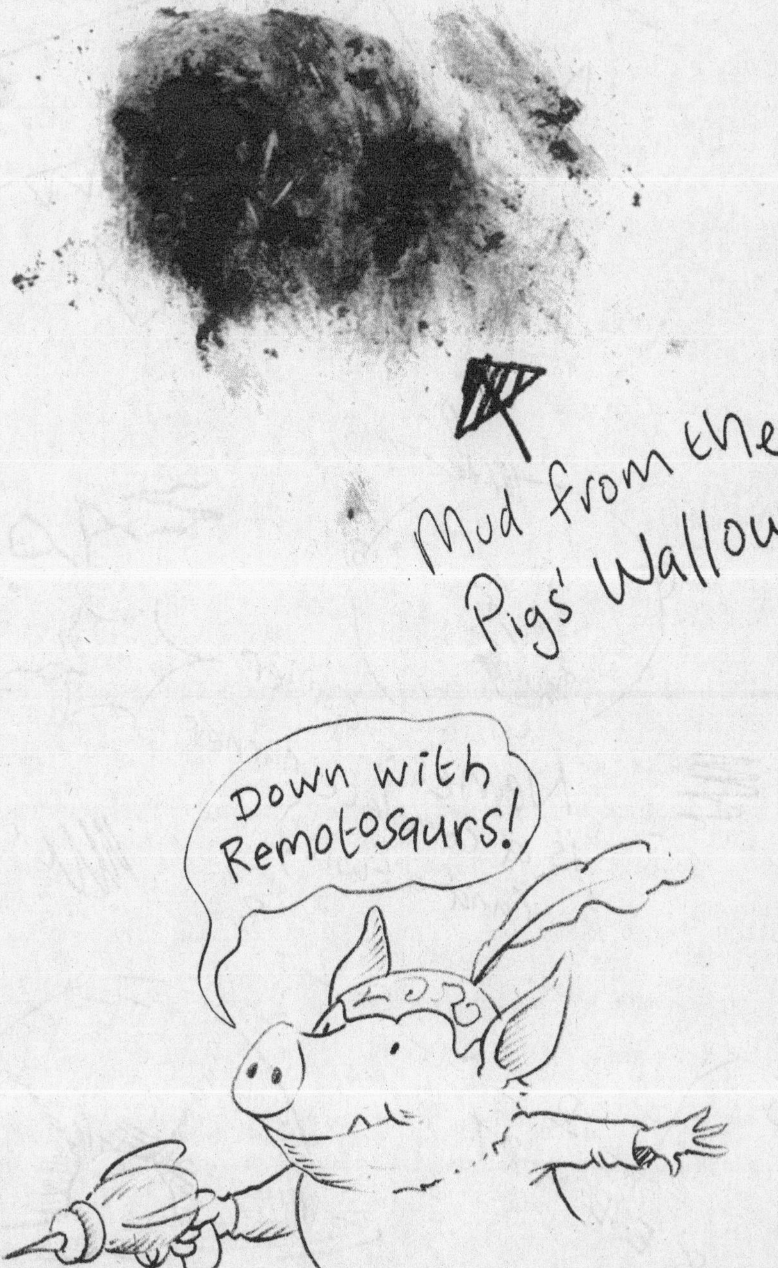
Mud from the Pigs' Wallow
Down with Remotosaurs!

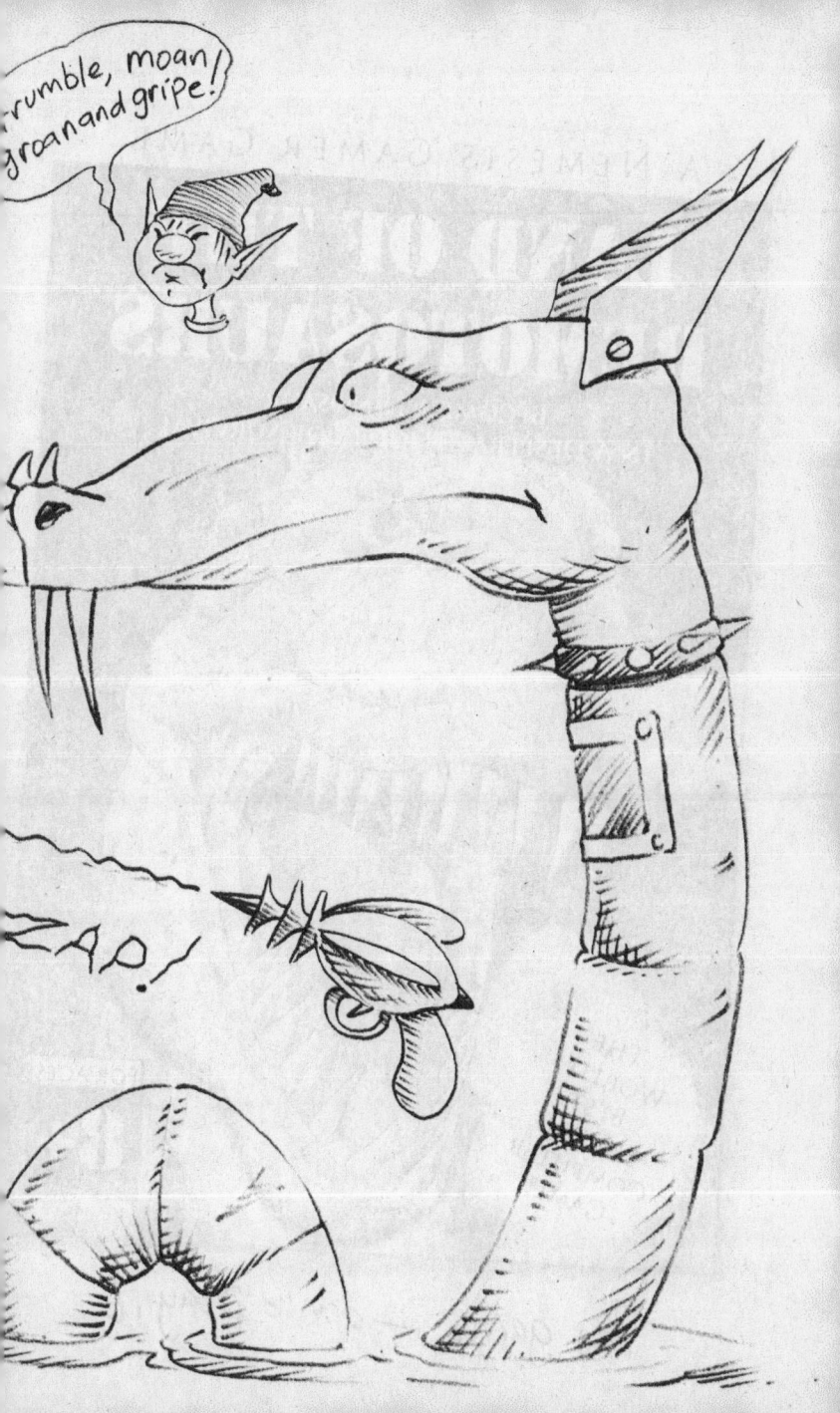

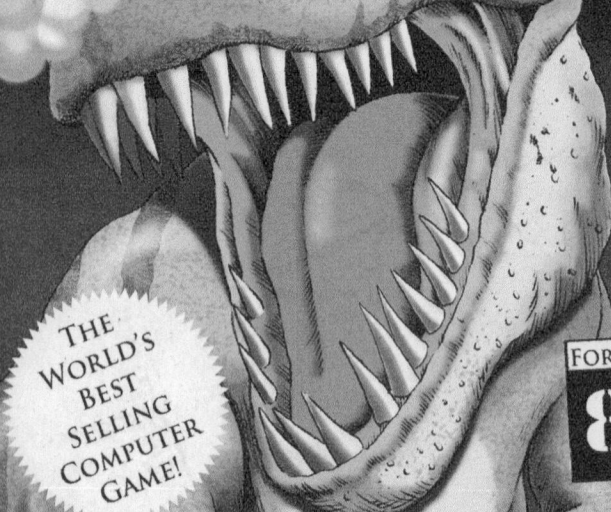

The game—don't play it